SABBATICA

SABBATICA

The Seas Of Death And The Arcana Of Death Bringer

As Compiled by Edgar Kerval

Nephilim Press

2013

SABBATICA
The Seas Of Death, And The Arcana Of Death Bringer
Edited by Edgar Kerval

Copyright 2013 to the individual authors and
artists featured within this work
ISBN: 978-0-9830639-7-1

Acknowledgements

Sabbatica emerges as an exposition of spectral seals, opening the astral paths of sorcery and magick. A convocation of a series of massive volumes, conjoined in arcane gnosis in order to evoke the primal path, that lead us to sacred knowledge pouring forth from secret vessels of sabbatic mysteries. This grimoire is an in-depth voyage to the waters of death, moving from anthropological to psychological and to the most hidden roots. Focused on the deep study and development of the patron of death, death deities, and necromantic rituals. It also contains Necrosophic and Qayanite traditions. *Sabbatica* would like to thank each one of the artists, writers and individuals who appear in this publication. Special thanks to my brother Phil Brito, Frank Redd and Nephilim Press for making this publication possible and the Red Gods for their infinite support and spiritual inspiration.

"Through The Seas Of Death

We emerge, as arcane seals

Now Broken, A Call To Death Gnosis

A Call To Hidden Mysteries

Always Veiled Beyond Human Consciousness"

Edgar Kerval
-2013-

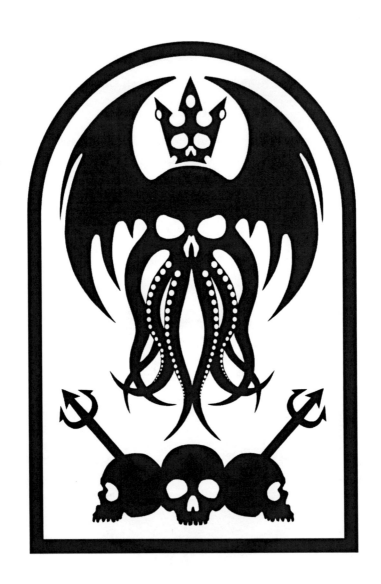

CONTENTS

The Death and Resurrection Show. 1

Sean Woodward
Dead...But Dreaming; The Arte Of Necromancy, And The Calling Of The Fallen. 13

S. Ben Qayin
Drawing Forth The Dead; The Necromantic Ritual of Re-Awakening 29

S. Ben Qayin
The Waters of Death and the Graveyard of Stars. 37

Nicholaj de Mattos Frisvold
Nathtantrika Pitra Paksha Puja (Honoring The Ancestors & Hallowed Dead). 51

Hermeticusnath (Aion 131)
The Last Touch of the Great Poisoner 59

Ljóssál Loðursson
The Crown Of Black Thorns: Explorations And Invocations Of Our Holy Mother Death 71

Edgar Kerval
The Triumph Of Death. 83

Claudio Carvalho
Arutam, Muisak, Nekas: "Three Souls Of The Shuar" 99

Andrew Dixon & Sarah Price

"In The Garden Of Bones: Working With Death & The Dead In
Pan-Aeonic Witchcraft".. 111

Bradley Allen Bennett
Death Magik And The Psychic Spiritual Nature Of Revenge 137

Dante Miel
-Seven Feet Under- The Heart of Fire beneath the Tongue of Silence 147

Kyle Fite
An Automatic Writing
Provocation: Justitia Omnibus 167

Robert Angelo Dalla Valle
Contributors 203

Visual Art

Dante Miel

    Spectrum 136

Sean Woodward

    Black Snake Ghuedhe Portal xvii

    Gros Bon Ange. 7

    Ti Bon Ange 11

Andrew Dixon & Sarah Price

    Authentic Jivaro Tsantsa 98

    Sigil Of Niantiel. 103

    Mattie 107

Saddie La Mort

    Triangle of EREBOS 112

    VGRS Square 117

    Triangle of NYX 122

Bradley Allen Bennett

    Seal of OAShA. 116

    Sigil of the Bird Serpent Goddess 131

Donnie Tincher

    Boneshrine. 110

Claudio Cesar Carvalho

    Voudon Atavism 81

Edgar Kerval

    Arcana Necrosofica. 12

Kyle Fite

    La Sirene. 36

    Tubal Cain 146

    Vulcanian Theophany 154

    Osiris 160

Kyle Fite & Kim Rogge Fite

    Gate Keeper 47

Ljóssál Loðursson

    Helstallr 58

Jekaira Damstra

    Offering To Kali 68

Orryelle Defenestrate Bascule

    Potentia. 27

    Bone Tripod. 89

    Mask 165

Vaenus Obscura

    Necromantic Triangle and circle 32

    La Santa Muerte 70

Hagen von Tulien

    Elements-fiery Death vii

    Primal Death god- viii

    ELEMENTAlS-Hearthy Death. xv

    Elements Liquid Death. 35

    Elements Grand Mort. 50

    Elements-Fiery Death. 57

    Custodians Of Death -La Santisima Muerte. 76

    Seal Of Transience 97

Seal of Finality. 145

Magick Kazin

Ghuedhe's Gate- xvi

Robert Angelo Dalla Valle

Pomba Gira da Calunga - One third of a triptych 166

Faces of MinXx. 180

Depth - Aphotic: Androctonus. 201

+ GHVÉÐHÉ'S GAҬE +

The Death and Resurrection Show

Sean Woodward

I. Deja-Vu-Vudu

"And lo, two Angels in White apparel sitting, the one at the head and the other at the foot, where the body of the Master had lain, who said: 'Why seek ye the living among the dead?'"

Here in the Adeptus Minor ritual of the Golden Dawn we encounter the two protagonists of the resurrection engine. It is in such inner rites of many mystery schools that we can see the ritual drama of the death and rebirth of the initiate. From the Pastos of Christian Rosencrutz to the Master Mason Degree can be found the allegory of rising from the pit of eternal sleep.

We can also see it in the Christian baptism ceremony where believers are born again, in the seasonal cycle of the Witchcraft celebrations and in the death and rebirth of Osiris. Nowhere is the personification of death more direct than in the exoteric and esoteric forms of Vudu. Perhaps only the Horsemen of the Apocalypse come close to this in-your-face, no-holds-barred reality.

The differences in attitude to the mysteries of death can be seen vividly in the funerary rites of a people. In the West we have managed to brush aside real acknowledgement of its reality, replacing it with sex and consumerism, with medicine and the surgeon's knife—with anything that will help us forget the inevitable. And yet it is interesting to see how we continue ancient practices, sometimes without even realizing what we are doing. We arrange photos of family members in groups, creating modern altars to our ancestors, to those who helped us with physical manifestation. We treasure an old watch, cufflinks or pen not just for their retro form, but for the memories of generations past, of loved ones departed, that they bring. In a world that increasingly attempts to glorify youth and the now, we find comfort in what has gone before.

With the Vudu Barons of the Cross and the Cemetery there is no denying the realms over which they have jurisdiction, no doubt about their nature. To walk with them is to understand the raw, brutal essence of being. The cult of death, of ancestor reverence is a major component of exoteric Vudu, but for all the possibilities of unearthly knowledge offered by such concourse, it is not the ear of these Lwa that we seek, for their work is more general in nature and it is the specific personal agents of resurrection that are our allies.

Whilst the Barons and the Ghuedhe family in particular are often feted by those seeking an understanding of the mysteries of death, it is, however, not these outward signs of the Death and Resurrection Show which have come to us down the ages that is of primary interest, rather it is the transformations at their heart which concern us, the personal impact upon the initiate and their relationship with Les Mysteries. For initiation is an unveiling of our own natures, of the lifetimes of work already undertaken and of the relationships we have forged in this world and beyond.

In exoteric Vudu there is a clear distinction between the realm of the living and that of the dead. In Haitian folklore there are many stories about ensuring that the dead remain dead and do not fall prey to the zombi-making powers of the Bokors, or workers of Red Magick. Ancestors are stored in the Govi pot, and after a year and a day, expensive rituals are undertaken to ensure they rise from the waters. Over time some of these ancestors may become themselves Lwa. In esoteric Vudu we look beyond these funerary rites to the very mechanics, means and maps of this process. In the long journey down the ages, the great magicians of Atlantis took care to encode the mysteries in totems, which would keep alive their work on the Earth as well as to ensure personal continuity of their efforts in future lifetimes. Their large-scale efforts ensured that sanctuaries were built at nexus points across the globe, that their inter-dimensional technologies were hidden and that a transmission of their teachings survived the destruction of their bodies. The greatest of them remained as Lwas, as Hoo and Doo spirits. Others continued to incarnate throughout the ages. There exist various levels of access to this knowledge throughout the later civilisations that they were instrumental in forming, as Michael Bertiaux states:

> *"The Sumerian levels of the transcendental id or Sumerian skandhas would serve to provide doorways for an exploration and entry into the Atlantean and Lemurian levels"*

It is in these levels, themselves remnants of older, stellar knowledge, that the magicians perfected the transmutations of both matter and their immaterial selves.

To enable this persistence of identity and mission requires the interaction of the Gros Bon Ange and the Ti Bon Ange. It is these great angels of being that are the principle players in the continual Death and Resurrection Show of the adept.

Of course many are familiar with the concept of a soul. In esoteric Vudu there is a deeper view, one which recognizes a dual nature to our higher selves and the distinct arenas of influence within which they operate. The Gros Bon Ange and the Ti Bon Ange bridge the realms of matter and spirit; they are vehicles of consciousness, which act as a conduit between the unseen realms and the realms of experience. Between them is a bond that unites that self which is outside the circles of time (the Ti Bon Ange) and that which carries the experiences of many lifetimes (the Gros Bon Ange) and retains the links with the Jean-Maine Familie of Spirits as well as those other lattices of energy fields which are pertinent to the development of the individual. The Ghuedhe Lwa are particularly of benefit as they have assisted the angels of many sorcerers in their education, in the journey between the worlds and in protecting ancient instruments of illumination from the profane. Some of these lattices can only be described by multi-dimensional magico meta-mathematics because they refer directly to the pre-Atlantean, trans-yuggothian spaces from where they came. Within these lattices are whole worlds that have been created by the activity of adepts. Due to the accumulation of knowledge and magickal sciences throughout these lifetimes, these treasuries remain between the worlds, whilst the angels act as guardians, waiting for the moment they can translate the maps to these places into the life stream of the adept. For this reason the maps to these spaces may manifest in a multitude of forms. They can become imprinted on consciousness as a result of a reverie; a form in clouds might suddenly suggest an insight or the work of another, bound into a book may offer the map that is required. The angels are ceaseless in their efforts to reveal that which has been hidden by the incarnation into flesh, to awaken the adept to his true identity and purpose.

It is by the practice of concentrated, directed thought that an environment conducive to their work can be created, which will allow the creative energies of the Gros Bon Ange to infiltrate our awareness. The practice of 'Digging the Grave', of enabling the Cosmic Leghba Logos to manifest through the Gros Bon Ange, is an ongoing, evolving activity. It is essential to the twin angels that the Great Work of the adept continues its unbroken course, for in the digging is the form of the Pastos uncovered. In the tomb of Christian Rosencrutz is seen a model of such magickal machines as might be employed to aid the twin angels in their duty. This drama of death and resurrection illustrates the symbolic methods of aligning consciousness in such a way as to be conducive to the revelations of the twin angels. In the past it has often taken a shock to jolt awake the beating of the adept. The physical re-enactment of death and resurrection, with the compliment of signs and teachings, has often created the paradigm shift necessary for the adept to recall his true nature.

In the words of the Chief Adept, who takes the place of Christian Rosencrutz and who rises from the tomb, is a clear understanding of the transformation that has taken place, for he states:

> "I am the purified. I have passed through the Gates of Darkness into Light. I have fought upon earth for Good. I have finished my Work. I have entered into the Invisible. I am the Lord of Life triumphant over Death. There is no part of me which is not of the Gods."

In the Tibetan descriptions of the Bardo there are clues to the understanding of the Death and Resurrection Show. For it is the quality of the light that is key to understanding that we have entered the realm of the dead. It also has to be remembered that not all rebirths may have happened on the Earth. There is a multitude of places within the material universe that have harbored our beings, much as the *Tibetan Book of the Dead* speaks of the realms an incarnation may pass into, of Hungry Ghosts and Gods, so they are the other realms beyond the Solar System, the trans-yuggothian places that have added to our experiences.

The primary role of our twin angels, however, is to help maintain consistency, to recover what has been lost to memory and to help us store the treasures of this lifetime for later retrieval.

There are other ways, unengaged instances, Deja-Vu-Vudu moments, when the Gros Bon Ange will break through the everyday consciousness to make itself known. These are often events that have not 'happened before', whose mix of circumstances, objects and participants could not have existed in any prior time. They are, however, examples of the Gros Bon Ange interceding because the knowledge gained from the Ti Bon Ange has shown the moment to be a crucial nexus point in the life of the aspirant, a crossroads in time and space where uncertainty multiplies and the effects of prior actions are magnified. It is in this crucible, this stirred cauldron of tangents that key moment choices will be made, courses of actions set in motion which will have a major impact upon events and the current life of the adept. And so the Gros Bon Ange possesses the consciousness for an instant, imparting the importance in the only way it can communicate, by creating a duplicate, a repeated moment, and a perception of something so similar that it triggers awareness in the fundamental pattern recognition routines of the brain. When this happens in the waking world, we experience it as Deja-vu. In the sleeping world the Gros Bon Ange is able to communicate this more easily, and we obtain the awareness known as lucid dreaming. In both instances it is the realization that something is wrong with the reality we inhabit that allows the Gros Bon Ange to startle our consciousness.

As the Gros Bon Ange intersects with the realms of the Lwa, it is able to communicate more easily through dreams. In extreme cases of jeopardy more than one Gros Bon Ange will work in unison to protect their hosts. An example is where real-time events are suddenly remembered to have been parts of a dream by one person which in turn triggers a memory of dreams in the second person quickly followed by an intense episode of Deja-Vu-Vudu so powerful that it forces them to dramatically change an element of their current activity and thus avoid any terminal outcomes that the Ti Bon Ange already had knowledge of. This is an example of a shared nexus point and demonstrates how the knowledge of these angels can be oracular and act as agents of change within the material universe.

By the practice of Voyance, of engaging with the spirits and Lwa with whom there is natural affinity, which has often been created from the relationships of previous lifetimes, we are able to enter into the secret storehouses, the totem treasures held in trust by the Gros Bon Ange over many lifetimes. These spirits of Voyance can take many forms and exist in many particular times and places. By a Pact of Voyance, an understanding that certain esoteric machines, certain mundane devices will be made known to the individual by the spirit, certain keys unique to the Vudu voyage of the individual made available. These keys belong to esoteric machines of illumination, which exist in the world of the Ti Bon Ange but are essential treasuries of the gnostic achievements and tools that the esoteric engineer has gathered over millennia. Some of the keys also function as triggers to enable the mind to dispel any clouds of forgetfulness, which the experience of being incarnated back into human form will have produced. For this reason, it is essential that the relationships between self, Gros Bon Ange and the Spirits of Voyance are maintained in good standing, that future incarnations may come to quick awareness of their true identity and role.

In the Golden Dawn symbolism of Christian Rosencrutz, an example of one of these triggers can be found.

> "Upon his breast was the Book T, a scroll explaining in full
> the mystic Tarot"

Elsewhere in the ritual, the rose of the Rose Croix is explained as having 22 petals, which represent the force of the 22 letters in nature. The Major Arcana of the Tarot also consists of 22 cards. It is clear that the *Book T*, or *Book of Thoth*, is an esoteric key encoded in pictorial form. It is an example of just one of the Atlantean engines preserved throughout the ages.

The importance of the relationship with the Spirits of Voyance cannot be emphasised enough because establishing the conditions which enable the direct knowledge and conversation of the Gros Bon Ange are difficult to create and in the early life of the incarnation, impossible to attain without the intellect to engage therein. It is necessary therefore for the Spirits of Voyance to exist in ways that will protect and direct the development of the incarnation until it is capable of independent movement and thought, of experiencing the keys, which trigger awareness and conversation with the Gross Bon Ange. In this way the Spirits of Voyance act as godparents to the soul, ensuring that its Vudu voyage remains on track at the earliest moment of the incarnation's new life.

II. A RITUAL OF REMEMBRANCE

It is in the cycle of Witchcraft celebrations that we find an auspicious time to dedicate our work with the agents of Voyance. On the night of All Hallows' Eve, having found a special crossroads location, we call upon the Sacred Twins to deepen our knowledge and conversation of the twin angels. In Crowley' *Liber ThIShARB*, some of the methods for attaining the magical memory are described. We take the instruments of our arte, the Mirroire Fantastique, we extend our arms and welcome Leghba, we draw the veves, we scatter rum and seeds and then we beseech the Twins with the following verses.

At the Crossroads I banish those
Dukes of Edom, that ruled in Chaos,
Lost Lords of the unbalanced force,
I call upon Leghba,
Lord of the Light and the Darkness.

Papa Marassa I call upon you
On All Hallow's Eve, dark and true
I walk backwards, I touch the earth
I gaze into the mirror
Searching, searching.
Bring me the treasures from before my birth
Papa Leghba open the doors beyond the Earth.

Papa Cemitiere I give offerings of food
Come undo my every move
Come change my clothes, come change my face
This night of the dead, where every place
Is a reflection of your world,
I trace the curled symbols of the veves
I heed the rituals of death
Scatter so many seeds
That they'd never be counted before dawn
I keep to the form of matter
And the form of the unseen.

This night is for the dead, for the Invisibles,
Ti Bon Ange, I call upon you,
Come speak from gilded glass
Tell me of the future and the past
I recount the names of my ancestors,
Stored in the Govi pot
Stored in the black Lwa stone
Show me those whose faces I have worn
Show me the days before I was born.

I ask that in the long night
Of my own new displacement
I will attain the state of invisibility
Bone will turn to light again.
Papa Marassa I call upon you
Come shine upon my face
Uncover the spaces
Of your treasures
Ride beneath the bright stars
Whisper the secrets of the cards
On the royal path home.

From the centre of the Earth,
From the Mountain of Initiation, of rebirth
From the chapel of Osiris Justified,
Make this my own true self
For I seek the alchemist's true wealth
Show me the path of Daleth, of the door,
The remembrance of all that has gone before.

III. Return to Ifa

Such a request to Les Mysteries will enable the lattices with which they inter-sect to enter into the life stream of the adept, for it is the same truths that are communicated in these stories of death and rebirth which have come down from ancient times and through a multitude of civilizations and practices.

SEAN WOODWARD

Continued reflection upon the tasks entrusted to the twin angels, the Marassas of being, will engage the vehicle of synchronicity and allow it to be operated by the twins.

In these relationships are many of the mysteries of gnosis, for the Vudu voyage is a two-sided coin. On the one hand, there is the purpose of the material universe, of the machinery of matter, to enable knowledge and experience of the senses. This is balanced by the link afforded by the two angels of the soul within the cosmic realms of Leghba, of the Perfected Adam. We continually fall into matter to delight in the joys of existence and rise into the Unseen, to know the reality of our being. By nurturing our connection with the Gros and Ti Bon Ange we ensure that we maintain a foot in both worlds as we walk the path to the mystical city of Ifa.

BIBLIOGRAPHY

Hurston, Zora Neale. Mules and Men. New York: Harper & Row, 1990

Regardie, Israel. The Golden Dawn. Llewellyn. St Paul, 1971

Bertiaux, Michael. Vudu Cartography. London: Fulgur, 2010

DEAD...BUT DREAMING; THE ARTE OF NECROMANCY, AND THE CALLING OF THE FALLEN

S. Ben Qayin

"Death, the inexorable and pitiless, is it but a release, the separation of the liberated spirit from the biologic matter? Or is death actually the final destruction, a total annihilation against the resurrection of a new life in the morning sun? Does death lead to the total darkness of the night or does it bring the vaunted light to the souls eagerly searching for the portals of eternal life?

~ DR. EMILE LAURENT, 'MAGICA SEXUALIS', 1934

T he realm of the Dead: The ethereal shadow land that lies parallel to the dense world of the living, just out of sight as a specter itself on the edge of breathing reality. It has been said that the fog-like barriers that separate our worlds can be magically worn down, and communication made possible with those who have crossed over into the cold twilight of un-death, still existing, though without the beat of a heart within their chests or the feel of warm blood running course through their now barren veins. The Dead are known to forever wander between the worlds, gliding in the shadows, thin as smoke, caressing the world of the living with their cold waif-like tendrils.

Magicians have long sought the council of the fallen Dead, seeking secret knowledge of lost and hidden things, of treasure and the forbidden future. Necromancy, or *Nekuomanteia [Greek]: Necro-* Dead, *Manteia-* Divination, has been practiced for thousands of years, being traced back to Babylonian Chaldea and Egypt, though has been most commonly recorded in Greek history. The first mention of Greek Necromancy was in Homer's *Odyssey* (700–650 B.C.E.), where Odysseus raised the Dead through the instruction of the Witch Circe.

Very little history of this 'Arte of the Dead' exists; so much is spread out over time and location. Of course, there is ancestor worship and the honoring of ancestors recorded in many lands, though it is not held in the same category as calling the dead forth for the sole purpose of divination, with the exceptions of religions such as Palo Mayombe, where it is quickly seen that ancestors *are* called forth from the Spirit World and employed for various reasons, including protection of oneself and home, and divination, which will be examined further on.

One of the main reasons Necromancy was practiced was to '*lay restless ghosts*'. That is, bring to peace Spirits who for some reason could not be content to go on with their existence in the Spirit World, and remained in that of the living. The Spirits would bring attention to their trouble at hand so it may be resolved, and they may finally rest. Necromancy eventually evolved to include divination and was practiced in places called Oracles of the Dead named '*Nekuomanteions*' that were generally located underground or within cemeteries or crypts of the deceased. These were secret gathering places that operated unseen from the condemning eyes of the masses, once Necromancy was seen as vulgar and outlawed. These Oracles were in such places that desolation knew well. They have always been in areas that Death frequents and casts His influence on, such as ancient battlefields, gallows trees, or in areas where violent death has occurred.

There have been noteworthy Magicians throughout history who have worked this forbidden 'Arte of the Dead', some unexpected, such as Jesus of Nazareth who rose Lazarus as well as others. Though I don't consider Jesus *(existing or not)* a true Necromancer, as he did not raise the dead for prophecy, but to show people that his father 'God' had chosen him to deliver God's holy word *(slavery)* to them. Of course, when one conjures the images of Necromancy, the famous scene depicting John Dee and Edward Kelly speaking with a Spirit in a cemetery, while inside a magical circle, comes to mind. However, truly it was not Dee, but Paul Warring in Walton-le-Dale, near Preston in Lancashire, who performed the rite with Kelly. One of the most detailed accounts of Necromancy comes from a rather celebrated Magician,

Eliphas Levi. Levi was hired by a rather mysterious woman dressed entirely in black with a black veil covering her face, who wished to call up the philosopher Magician, Apollonius of Tyan. Levi writes of his amazing experience raising the Spirit,

> "...I was clothed in a white garment, very similar to the alb of our Catholic priests, but longer and wider, and I wore upon my head a crown of vervain leaves, intertwined with a golden chain. I held a new sword in one hand, and in the other the ritual. I kindled two fires with the requisite prepared substances, and began reading the evocations of the ritual in a voice at first low, but rising by degrees...the smoke spread, the flame' caused the objects upon which it fell to waver, then it went out, the smoke still floating white and slow about the marble alter; I seemed to feel a quaking of the earth, my ears tingled, my heart beat quickly. I heaped more twigs and perfumes on the chafing-dishes, and as the flame again burst up, I beheld distinctly, before the alter, the figure of a man of more than normal size, which dissolved and vanished away. I recommenced the evocations and placed myself within a circle which I had drawn previously between the tripod and the altar. Thereupon the mirror which was behind the alter seemed to brighten in its depth, a man's form was outlined therein, which increased and seemed to approach by degrees. Three times, and with eyes closed, I invoked Apollonius. When I again looked forth there was a man in front of me, wrapped from head to foot in a species of shroud, which seemed more grey than white.

> "He was lean, melancholy and beardless, and did not altogether correspond to my preconceived notion of Apollonius. I experienced an abnormally cold sensation, and when I endeavored to question the phantom I could not articulate a syllable. I therefore placed my hand upon the sign of the pentagram, and pointed the sword at the figure, commanding it mentally to obey and not alarm me, in virtue of the said sign. The form thereupon became vague, and suddenly disappeared. I directed it to return, and presently

*felt, as it were, a breath close by me; something touched my
hand which was holding the sword, and the arm became
immediately benumbed as far as the elbow. I divined that
the sword displeased the spirit, and I therefore placed its
point downwards, close by me, within the circle. The human
figure reappeared immediately, but I experienced such an
intense weakness in all my limbs, and a swooning sensation
came so quickly over me that I made two steps to sit down,
whereupon I fell into a profound lethargy, accompanied by
dreams, of which I had only a confused recollection when I
came again to myself. For several subsequent days my arm
remained benumbed and painful. The apparition did not
speak to me, but it seemed that the questions I had designed
to ask answered themselves in my mind..."* ~ Eliphas Levi,
Transcendental Magic: Its Doctrine and Ritual, 1896

Ironically, Apollonius practiced Necromancy himself by raising the famous Spirit of Achilles. Unlike most Necromantic rites, he did not perform
a rite at all, and offered none of the traditional libations to bring forth the
Spirit. Instead, he offered but a simple prayer or calling to the Ghost,

*"O Achilles, most of mankind declares that you are dead, but
I cannot agree with them, nor can Pythagoras my spiritual
ancestor. If then we hold to the truth, show to us your form;
for you would not profit not a little by showing yourself to
my eyes, if you should be able to use them to attest to your
existence."*

Traditionally, there are several different methods for evoking the Dead,
or holding congress with them in the Underworld. One method stems from
the honoring of ancestors by way of libation of various substances. This account of practice is detailed in Homer's *Odyssey* where Odysseus *(as mentioned)* raises the Spirit Tiresias; a blind prophet who would reveal the future
of his *(Odysseus)* journeys, who dwells in Hades. When in the Underworld,
Odysseus begins his Necromantic Arte by first digging a sacrificial pit to
hold the libations to be used. Once done, he pours a mixture of milk and
honey around the pit, followed by sweet wine and finally fresh spring water,
all of which are in the end, sprinkled over with barley. When all libations
have circled the sacrificial pit, a prayer is given to the Dead pledging them

upon returning to the world of the living, the best sterile heifer of the heard, and 'treasures' to be burnt upon a pyre in their honor. Once this recitation has commenced, a separate and personalized prayer is offered to the Spirit, in Odysseus' case, Tiresias, that promises *(again, upon his safe return)* the sacrifice of an all-black ram. At last, with a bronze sword, he bleeds two black sheep of opposing sex into the prepared sacrificial pit, at which point the Dead appear and draw near to quench their thirst and obtain the strength and life energy that lies within the spilt blood. Odysseus is in need of the bronze sword to keep the Spirits at bay, keeping them clear of the blood which gives them the ability to speak and have tangibility. Odysseus proclaims to the restless Dead,

> *"With my sharp sword again unsheathed I watched over the pit of sacrificial blood, lest any of the fragile dead draw near that blood before I met Tiresias."*

Only is Tiresias allowed to partake of the blood so that intended interaction may occur. This use of a sword in Necromancy is largely reminiscent of Levi's already given account, and is a recurring theme or element within this praxis. It is interesting to note that a physical sword, surly being magical, has the ability to harm a spiritual entity. This belief is also a central theme in Arabic mysticism concerning Djinn.

The use of Blood Sorcery in Necromancy is also very important. Blood is a vital power source to be used by the Dead to appear and communicate. Though there are other rites of evoking the Dead, they generally take many days to gather the needed energy for the Spirit to appear. However, when blood is utilized, its energy is so strong that the Dead can easily draw from it what they require for interaction with the Magician almost immediately.

Blood Sorcery has been practiced since man began to use Magic. A true Magician naturally feels and understands that this personal substance that gives us life is powerful without equal. It is the ultimate sacrifice when given, the ultimate energy source for Spirits of all kinds to draw from, and the Magician's personal life signature. It is the Spirit in material form, the 'Philosophers Stone' of crimson red. I have written on this subject at length in a piece titled, *"The Arte Of Blood"* featured in "Qliphoth" Opus II, so I will not go on here, except to reinforce the necessity of this vital liquid in rites concerning quickly drawing forth the fallen Dead.

Another interesting example of Necromancy resides in Lovecraft's work, *The Case of Charles Dexter Ward*, where Ward recites a Necromantic evocation to raise his ancestor. The rite involves Yog-Sothoth as the 'Keeper of the Crossroads'. Whether fact or fancy, it is interesting none the less. The rite involves having the 'salts' or ashes of the deceased and reading an evocation. The use of 'salts' in Necromancy has been described by Borellus, a seventeenth century philosopher/alchemist,

> "*The essential Saltes of Animals may be so prepared and preserved, that an ingenious Man may have the whole Ark of Noah in his own Studie, and raise the fine Shape of an Animal out of its Ashes at his Pleasure; and by the lyke Method from the essential Saltes of humane Dust, a Philosopher may, without any criminal Necromancy, call up the Shape of any dead Ancestour from the Dust where into his Bodie has been incinerated.*" ~ Borellus

The evocation to raise the Dead is as follows,

> "*Per Adonai Eloim, Adonai Jehova, Adonai Sabaoth, Metraton On Agla Mathon, verbum pythonicum, mysterium salamandrae, conventus sylvorum, antra gnomorum, daemonia Coeli God, Almonsin, Gibor, Jehosua, Evam, Zariatnatmik, veni, veni, veni.*
> *(Said in repetition for two hours),*
>
> *DIES MIES JESCHET BOENE DOESEF DOUVEMA ENITEMAUS !*
>
> *Yi-nash-Yog-Sothoth-he-lgeb-fi-throdog-Yah !*
>
> *Y'AI 'NG'NGAH,*
>
> *YOG-SOTHOTH,*
>
> *H'EE-L'GEB,*
>
> *F'AI THRODOG,*
>
> *UAAAH !*"

And to lay the Dead to rest again, the evocation is repeated, with the omission of the last section to be replaced with,

"OGTHROD AI'F,

GEB'L—EE'H,

YOG-SOTHOTH,

'NGAH'NG AI'Y,

ZHR !"

There are other lengthier methods of calling the Dead forth; this next example is again related by Levi, though I hesitate to quote here as it is lengthy, but find it such an exact description of this specific Arte of the Dead, that I have decided to include it here for those who are in need of this information and wish to follow its example. The ceremony/ritual is accessible from a LHP point of view, as there are no Holy orations or devotions given to the Demiurge. Where such is needed or wanted, the Magician applies patron deities as they desire. This rite is designed to focus on the Spirit being called forth, not on a Deity or the Magician himself/herself. The procedure is as follows:

> *"We must, in the first place, carefully collect the memorials of him (or her) whom we desire to behold, the articles he used, and on which his impressions remains; we must also prepare an apartment in which the person lived, or otherwise, one of similar kind, and place his portrait veiled in white therein, surrounded with his favorite flowers, which must be renewed daily. A fixed date must then be observed, either the birthday of the person, or that day which was most fortunate for his and our own affection, one of which we may believe that his soul, however blessed elsewhere, cannot lose the remembrance; this must be the day for the evocation and we must provide for it during the space of fourteen days. Throughout this period we must refrain from extending to anyone the same proofs of affection which we have the right to expect from the dead; we must observe strict chastity, live in retreat, and take only modest and light collation daily.*
>
> *Every evening at the same hour we must shut ourselves in the chamber consecrated to the memory of the lamented person, using only one small light, such as that of a funeral lamp or taper. This light should be placed behind us, the portrait*

should be uncovered and we should remain before it for an hour, in silence; finally, we should fumigate the apartment with a little good incense, and go out backwards. On the morning of the day fixed for the evocation, we should adorn ourselves as if for a festival, not salute anyone first, make but a single repast of bread, wine, and roots, or fruits; the cloth should be white, two covers should be laid, and one portion of the bread broken should be set aside; a little wine should also be placed in the glass of the person we design to invoke.

The meal must be eaten alone in the chamber of evocations, and in the presence of the veiled portrait; it must be all cleared away at the end, except the glass belonging to the dead person, and his portion of bread, which must be placed before the portrait. In the evening, at the hour for the regular visit, we must repair in silence to the chamber, light a fire of cypress wood, and cast incense seven times thereon, pronouncing the name of the person whom we desire to behold. The lamp must then be extinguished, and the fire permitted to die out. On this day the portrait must not be unveiled. When the flame is extinct, put more incense on the ashes, and invoke God according to the forms of the religion to which the dead person belonged, and according to the ideas which he himself possessed of God. While making this prayer we must identify ourselves with the evoked person, speak as he spoke, believe in a sense as he believed; then, after a silence of fifteen minutes, we must speak to him as if he were present, with affection and with faith, praying him to manifest to us.

Renew this prayer mentally, covering the face with both hands; then call him thrice with a loud voice; tarry on our knees, the eyes closed and covered, for some minutes; then call again thrice upon him in a sweet and affectionate tone, and slowly open the eyes. Should nothing result, the same experiment must be renewed in the following year, and if necessary a third time, when it is certain that the desired apparition will be obtained, and the longer it has been delayed the more realistic and striking it will be."

"Evocations of knowledge and intelligence are made with more solemn ceremonies. If concerned with a celebrated personage, we must meditate for twenty-one days upon his life and writings, form an idea of his appearance, converse with him mentally, and imagine his answers; carry his portrait, or at least his name, about us; follow a vegetable diet for twenty-one days, and a severe fast during the last seven. We must next construct the magical oratory. This oratory must be invariably darkened; but if we operate in the daytime, we may leave a narrow aperture on the side where the sun will shine at the hour of the evocation, and place a triangular prism before the opening, and a crystal globe, filled with water, before the prism. If the operation be arranged for the night the magic lamp must be so placed that its single ray shall be upon the alter smoke. The purpose of the preparations is to furnish the magic agent with elements of corporeal appearance, and to ease as much as possible the tension of imagination, which could not be exalted without danger into the absolute illusion of dream.

For the rest, it will be easily understood that a beam of sunlight, or the ray of a lamp, colored variously, and falling upon curling and irregular smoke, can in no way create a perfect image. The chafing-dish containing the sacred fire should be in the center of the oratory, and the alter of perfumes close by. The operator must turn toward the east to pray, and the west to invoke; he must be either alone or assisted by two persons preserving the strictest silence; he must wear the magical vestments, which we have described in the seventh chapter and must be crowned with vervain and gold. He should bathe before the operation, and all his under garments must be of the most intact and scrupulous cleanliness. The ceremony should begin with a prayer suited to the genius of the spirit about to be invoked and one which would be approved by him if he still lived. For example, it would be impossible to evoke Voltaire by reciting prayers in the style of St. Bridget. For the great men of antiquity, we may see the hymns of Cleathes or Orpheus, with the adjuration terminating the Golden Venus of Pythagoras. In our own evocation of Apollonius, we used the magical philosophy of Patricius for the ritual, containing the doctrines of Zoroaster and the writings of Hermes Trismegistus. We recited the Nuctemeron of Apollonius in Greek with a loud voice and added the following conjuration,

"Vouchsafe to be present, O Father of All, and thou Thrice Mighty Hermes, Conductor of the dead. Asclepius son of Hephaistus, Patron of the Healing Art; and thou Osiris, Lord of strength a vigor, do thou thyself be present too. Arnebascenis, Patron of Philosophy, and yet again Asclepius, son of Imuthe, who presidest over poetry.

Apollonius, Apollonius, Apollonius, Thou teachest the Magic of Zoroaster, son of Oromasdes; and this is the worship of the Gods." ~ Eliphas Levi, Transcendental Magic: Its Doctrine and Ritual, 1896

When looking at the use of libations in connection with honoring the Dead in this example, the Afro-Brazilian spiritual traditions again come to mind, though I will not go into detail here, as there are other skilled Magicians who are covering this subject in length within this compilation. What I will do in place, is shortly examine a related practice of honoring the Dead and working with them in the form of the recently surfaced, though long practiced, Qayinitic tradition of honoring ancestors of Spirit, rather than of blood *(unless applicable)*, which draws its power from praxis very similar to that of the Afro-Brazilian traditions, as well as from Traditional Western Ceremonial structures. In the Holy text of *Liber Falxifer,* we see a great fusing of these two different and ancient magical systems into one very solid and powerful manifestation.

Within the Qayinite tradition, libations are given in honor of Holy Qayin, Lord of Death at 12:00 a.m. every Monday night. Offerings of Incense, Liquor, Water, Tobacco, Bread, Flowers and Blood are given to the Rebellious One. These offerings are very similar to the ancient offerings given by the already mentioned Odysseus to the Dead,

"When in the underworld, Odysseus begins his Necromantic Arte by first digging a sacrificial pit to hold the libations to be used. Once done he pours a mixture of milk and honey around the pit, followed by sweet wine and finally fresh spring water, all of which are in the end, sprinkled over with barley."

It is believed by the Cult of Death, *"Templum Falcis Cruentis"*, that Qayin is the son of Samael, and as such they are in relation, His son/daughter. However, this lineage does not flow in the form of blood, but of Spirit. In other words, one who is born into a family of Christians can still be of the Holy Blood of Qayin. The link is not a physical one, but one ethereal on the plane of Spirit. Once those of Qayin pass on, they are able to be accessed and worked with as guiding and protective Spirits, assisting the Magician in a great many tasks and situations.

Qayin is also seen as 'The Lord of Death', for the slaying of His brother, clay born Abel. He is known as 'the first tiller of the Earth, and first killer of man'. Thus, all of Death's attributes are assigned to Him. Of course as mentioned, there is the Holy Bloodline of Qayin that has passed on into the Spirit realm. When working with the Holy Dead, they must be treated with great honor and respect.

I must say that I am not officially involved with the Temple, but follow many of its recorded traditions. I offer this information only as an overview and study of the Cult of Death and its practices, and not as an official member relaying teachings. I in no way am speaking against the Cult; I honor their ways. However, I also hold the belief that one needs not be an official member of anything, if one is born of the energetic current naturally.

When one begins to contemplate Necromancy, generally it is thought that only the Spirit is brought forth in ritual to commune with. However, there are cases where the 'dead' body is again infused with a sort of life and spirit, so that communication may be achieved with the living. One ancient Greek example is a tale by Lucan titled *Pharsalia*, 65 C.E., where the character Erictho reanimates the corpse of a Pompeian soldier by pumping hot blood into it along with magical herbs. Barbarous words are then spoken followed by the evocation of various Underworld deities, causing the soldier's Spirit to appear. The Spirit refuses to possess his now rotting corpse, but is forced inside by the lashings of a snake wielded by Erictho, and with threats to the Spirit concerning the Underworld, which is very reminiscent of the use of '*The Spirit Chain*' in Goetic work, also being of Greek origin.

As well, there is the use of skulls in the Necromantic rites of the Greeks, which is also used in the sacred rites in connection with the Dead, being used as 'Oracles' for divination, within the praxis of the "*Templum Falcis Cruentis*". And though there is a history of this, it has been covered well recently in Daniel Schulke's, *Veneficium*, and I don't wish to repeat what has already been given.

This idea of a magically revived corpse would fall under the classification of a 'Zombie', or the re-animated Dead. These 'Dead' are brought back to animation magically through various secret rites. Haiti is long known for its history of Walking Dead. William Seabrook, who was an old drinking friend of Aleister Crowley, speaks about tales he had heard of Zombies working in sugar fields under the light of the moon while black smoky Spirits circled overhead. Unlike the examples of Greek and English corpse re-animation, the Haitian 'Zombie' was said to be soulless and unable to speak, thus making it useless for divination.

> "...Zombies prayed neither to Papa Legba nor to Brother Jesus, for they were dead bodies walking, without souls or minds"..."But the Zombies shuffled through the marketplace, recognizing neither father nor wife, nor mother, and as they turned leftward up the path leading to the graveyard, a woman whose daughter was in the procession of the dead, threw herself screaming before the girls shuffling feet and begged her to stay; but the grave-cold feet of the daughter and the feet of the other dead shuffled over her and onward; and as they approached the graveyard, they began to shuffle faster and rushed among the graves, and each before his own empty grave began clawing at the stones and earth to enter it again; and as their cold hands touched the earth of their own graves, they fell and lay there, rotting carrion." ~ W.B. Seabrook, *The Magic Island*, 1929

I must include Seabrook's own personal experience of meeting three 'Zombies' in a sugar field in the middle of the day, simply because it is so fantastic,

"My first impression of the three supposed 'Zombies', who continued dumbly at work, was that there was something about them unnatural and strange. They were plodding like brutes, like automatons. Without stooping down, I could not fully see their faces, which were bent expressionless over their work. Polynice touched one of them on the shoulder, motioned him to get up. Obediently, like an animal, he slowly stood erect – and what I saw then, coupled with what I had heard previously, or despite it, came as a rather sickening shock. The eyes were the worst. It was not my imagination. They were in truth like the eyes of a dead man, not blind, but staring, unfocused, unseeing. The whole face, for that matter, was bad enough. It was vacant, as if there was nothing behind it. It seemed not only expressionless, but incapable of expression. I had seen so much previously in Haiti that was outside ordinary normal experience that for the flash of a second I had a sickening, almost panicky lapse in which I thought, or rather felt, 'Great God', maybe this stuff is really true, and if it is true, it is rather awful, for it upsets 'everything'. By 'everything' I meant the natural fixed laws and processes on which all modern human thought and actions are based." ~ W.B. Seabrook, The Magic Island, 1929

Another fantastic personal account of Necromancy that occurred in Africa which involved the evocation of the Spirit of a fallen king *(that acted as solid re-animated flesh)* is given by Frederick Kaigh in his 1947 book, *Witchcraft and Magic of Africa*. He describes a ceremony he witnessed of a tribe that had lost its king, and needed to evoke him to ask who should be appointed to the then vacant throne. This small series of excerpts speaks of the kings' sudden appearance and the authors amazed reaction in response:

"Nkatosi, the chief with whose corpse I had but a few hours since encountered so much trouble, is sitting quite unconcernedly on his throne. I did not see him come, but I saw him there as plainly as I can this sunny afternoon see the policeman on his beat outside my window. Everyone present sees him as clearly as I do."..."With all too vivid memories of the recently seen, vile and stinking corpse, I feel none too well at this demonstration."..."For the first time he rises, and for the first time, his feet actually touch the earth. After that he makes no more sound, and from that moment he gradually begins to look less

material as it were. He turns away from the people to face the moon, and it is then that, for the first time, we see the dim outline of the horrid bashed-in wound in the back of the skull. He walks slowly and majestically down the lane of the moon, and thus, naturally and simply, sets out on his long lost journey." ~ *Frederick Kaigh,* Witchcraft and Magic of Africa, *1947*

Though this is clearly an account of true Necromancy, the Spirit called forth was able to take on a completely solid form without entering its physical 'dead' body. This is reminiscent of Levi's account of the seeing and being touched by the Spirit Apollonius in full physical form. These examples should be seen and remembered as a warning to the Magician, as to the strength the Dead possess and wield.

There are other dangers to be warned of. When working with the Dead, some ancient Necromancers believed they must meet them *'halfway'*, that is, in a middle ground between the world of the living, and that of the dead. They would leave their body in order to travel to the Underworld, or close to it. The danger presented here is the Magicians being drawn too close the Spirit world, and then not having the strength to return to their living bodies, thus being fated to join the ranks of the Dead themselves. As well, let us not forget the warning words of Lovecraft's Necromancer, Jedediah Orne of Salem,

> *"I say to you againe, does not call up Any that you can not put down; by the which I meane, Any that can in Turne call up somewhat against you, whereby your Powerfullest Devices may not be of use. Ask of the Lesser, least the Greater shall not wish to answer, and shall commande more than you."* ~ *H.P. Lovecraft, The Case of Charles Dexter Ward, 1943*

I have felt that a bit of background was needed on this subject of Necromancy, though I also wish to contribute to this forbidden Arte in the form of a single ritual derived from ancient traditions, and infused with new concepts. Looking at Necromancy through scientific/magical eyes, I analyze the mechanics of the Arte and look to isolate the methods *(that resonate with me)* that make it work. As Frazier would say,

> *"...to draw out the few simple threads of which the tangled skein is composed; to disengage the abstract principles from their concrete applications; in short, to discern the spurious science behind the bastard art."* ~ *The Golden Bough, 1890*

I have found that, as with most all rituals, it is the culminating of energy that ensures the success of a Necromantic rite. One must have obtained, or generated, enough power to reach through the barriers of the worlds and make contact with the entity intended. Often times, this is done before the ritual even begins, though through ritual, great energy is also brought up and directed at the intended contact and communication. It is known that adjusting one's energy to a specific current is also of great help in ensuring this success. As an example, when working with Lovecraftian Entities, one should immerse themselves in that particular current by reading Lovecraft, meditating in twilight while speaking the entities names with intent to be heard, and of course practicing various forms of Lovecraftian *'Fringe'* Magic, such as is presented in *Volubilis Ex Chaosium.*

When working with the Death Current, one must align themselves with this energy as well. Personally because I work with Chthonic Spirits regularly, I wear a 300-year-old coffin nail around my neck at all times, to help me keep in touch with this current. As well, when working with the Dead and Chthonic Spirits, I use an oak wand that was ritually harvested from an ancient gallows tree. These items in combination with other 300-year-old coffin nails, graveyard soil and bones of the Fallen, create a concentration of Death energy that powers any rite involving communication with the Dead.

Necromancy is a little known art, leaving many areas open for the Necromancer to experiment with and study. Its history is ancient and hidden, shrouded away from the light of normalcy and 'Natural Law'. There are many reasons one would utilize this dark art, but perhaps its use is truly based on our curiosity to know what lies ahead of us. For the darkness will indeed come and claim us all, we are in this very moment being stalked by Death. He is behind you, to your left. And, once we are *'gone'*, perhaps someone will call us up, ask us of our knowledge, of our times and life. The following ritual is accessible to all who wish to utilize it. However, in the great spirit of Lovecraft, this rite is also intended for my personal use...I ask the ancestors of my true bloodline, that I call to through these written words, across the seas of time that now separate us, to use this ritual to call me up once I have *'gone'*, to raise me from this blackened earth once again...for I will come...

Drawing Forth the Dead; The Necromantic Ritual of Re-Awakening

S. Ben Qayin

The Necromantic ritual being presented here is based on the various methods of Necromancy discussed throughout this piece. It brings together the effective elements needed to generate the power to push through the barriers that lie between the world of the living and that of the Dead. It is designed to raise a great amount of energy, while simultaneously descending the Necromancer into a deep state of consciousness. In this manner, the Necromancer is ritually descending down into the Underworld, while the Dead are being raised up from out of it, creating a ritual space of twilight, *'halfway'* between the worlds.

This ritual should be held indoors in a large area, or partially indoors if there are holes in the roofing and walls. It should take place somewhere abandoned, forgotten with time, somewhere deserted or decayed where memories linger as dust upon an untrodden floor. A place like a forgotten warehouse, in the basement of an old house, in the attic of a strange factory, somewhere that is scarcely frequented, but that once was, would be ideal.

The Necromantic Circle is best made using white chalk, as it will not be disturbed when the Necromancer travels the descending staircase into 'the spaces between', though crushed eggshells or flour may be utilized. The circle is 12ft. in diameter. At 4 ½ ft in from the outer edge of the circle, another circle is drawn with a diameter of 3ft. All edges of the inner circle should be 4 ½ ft, from the edges of the outer circle, placing it in the direct center of the larger circle. Locate the North of the large circle using a compass, and begin a spiral pattern counter-clockwise or widdershins around the inside of the large circle three times, ending at the North edge of the smaller circle. Starting again at the top or North edge of the large circle where the spiral begins, start sectioning off areas as you travel the spiral inward, making each section slightly smaller than the last. The last section should not be smaller than the size of the Necromancer's foot. On each of the sections or steps, a pentagram is to be drawn so that they face the inner circle the Necromancer is to work in. This is done to infuse the circle with energy and strength. From the inside of the inner circle looking out, the Necromancer is surrounded by empowering pentagrams, while from outside the circle, they are seen as protective pentacles.

When done, the circle creates the illusion of a descending spiral staircase that ends in a small circular 3ft. area, where the Magician will call up the Dead and hold congress with whichever Spirit he has called forth.

The Necromantic Triangle of Evocation should also be drawn out with white chalk as mentioned with the circle. And like the circle, it also measures 12ft. from its apex pentagram (turned facing the North of the circle), to its base lying between the two adjacent pentagrams that help form the second and third points of the triangle *(see illustration)*. Once the Necromantic Triangle has been drawn, a 3ft. circle is to be drawn centered inside. This is known as the Spirit Circle where libations of blood are offered.

This rite represents the journey into the Underworld, the descent into darkness, into an un-natural silence, where the Necromancer travels into the land of the Dead, and is able to hear their gossamer whispers. This symbolic descent into the Underworld is reminiscent of the ancient rite of walking a labyrinth, as Thomas Karlsson points out,

> *"The paths of the labyrinth will deeply influence the mind. It is claimed that these labyrinths are pictures of the mind and the brain. To enter these ancient stone labyrinths is a form of initiation. It stages an entry into the centre of the Underworld where the core of the soul and secret of existence; the diamond, can be found."~ Thomas Karlsson, Uthark: Nightside of the Runes, 2002*

The praxis of Traveling around the Magical Circle counterclockwise, or widdershins, is drawn from an inversion of an ancient rite practiced in

Freemasonry called 'Circumambulation'. An initiate is led around the temple clockwise three times to honor the 'Grand Architect' of the Universe. Here where it is used, it represents the un-natural flow of natural laws, and in effect, is a direct rebellious act directed at the 'Grand Architect'. Bringing the Dead back to life is an un-natural act and not what is 'meant to be'. Necromancy goes against the Natural Order. It is interesting to note that this act of 'Circumambulation' has been traced back to ancient Pagan Roman times, making its utilization here a complementary fit.

Libations of milk and honey, blood, red roses, and myrrh incense are to be given in two different ways depending on your location. If outside, pour the mixture of milk and honey around the pit or Spirit Circle dug in the Triangle. The blood of course is to be drained into the earthen pit, and the roses are to be placed around the very edge of the pit. If inside, pour the mixture of milk and honey around the Spirit Circle designated for the offerings. Once done, utilize a clean black bowl for the blood offered, and place it in the center of the Spirit Circle surrounded by the red roses. The myrrh incense should be burning just inside all three points of the Necromantic Triangle, and there should be enough placed there to burn for a good length of time. An oak wand, scepter is needed for this rite, as oak is the wood of the Crossroads. As well, if you are contacting a specific Spirit, some of their personal belongings are to be placed within the Necromantic Triangle.

As tradition would have it, a sword is utilized as well to protect the Necromancer of unwanted Spirits, and drive off those who would do harm.

Begin the rite at midnight. The Necromantic Circle and Triangle as well as all offerings should already be in their place, and all incense lit. Use whatever candles are necessary to provide dim lighting. Begin standing outside of the circle, facing its North side, so your back is to the triangle. Once there, take a deep breath, and know it is the last one you will take in the world of the living, until you again return outside of the circle. When your mind is clear of all internal dialogue, begin by taking your first step. As each step is taken, trace over the pentagrams on each step with your oak scepter infusing them with power. The Magician slows his breathing, clears his mind, and sinks into a deeper level of consciousness with each step, so that when finally arriving at the inner/bottom platform of calling, he is attuned to the energy

VENVS OBSCVRA MMXII

being worked with, and ready to begin the rite. The journey 'down' should be slow and steady.

Once at the bottom, in the Circle of Calling, sit down, close your eyes and meditate on the blackness that surrounds you. Your wand should be in your left hand, your sword in your right. Feel the cold of the night upon your skin, feel the Spirits of the Underworld already begin to draw near in anticipation of the rite shortly to begin. Open your eyes and call to them, bring them forth, though they can be dangerous, their presence strengthens the rite. The words are whispered softly with Intent, not forceful with Will. They are spoken slowly with meaning. When you feel it is time, begin,

> "Dark Spirits of forever night,
> Sinestral Shades of liquid soot,
> Hear my words...
> I call you...
> Gather round from forsaken nether realms,
> Draw near...
> Know the warmth of my living voice upon your cold dead lears,
> Know my Spirit that calls yours from across the Void,
> Phantasmal whispers of Twilight's Shade,
> Hear my words...
> I call you...
> Lost Specters of Midnight's Garden,
> Damned Souls of Luna's light,
> Draw near...
> For the Darkness that ever surrounds you..,
> Is ever within me..."

Once spoken three times with devotion, the Necromancer is ready to call forth the intended Spirit of their choosing. Here I leave it to the Necromancer to develop their own oration to the lost one they wish to speak with. It is important to remember to be direct with your wording, and patient for a response. Upon completion of the rite, thank the Spirit for attending and working with you, inform it that you have no more to say at this time, and that it is again free to wander in the mists. When you feel it has departed, stand and address the Chthonic Spirits that still surround and thank them for attending as well, but that you now ask them to depart and to do you no harm, as you are protected under the name of the Dark One, Samael.

Proceed slowly back 'up' the stairs to the living world of man. As each step is taken, slowly raise your consciousness from out of the meditative state it has been in. Before leaving the circle make the sign of the pentagram in the air in front of you, and cross back out of the Necromantic Circle. The rite is finished...

A/P   LA SIRENE

THE WATERS OF DEATH AND THE GRAVEYARD OF STARS

Nicholaj de Mattos Frisvold

"The power of death signifies that this real world can only have a neutral image of life, that life's intimacy does not reveal its dazzling consumption until the moment it gives out."

~GEORGES BATAILLE

There is a Haitian proverb that tells us: 'we are all dead, just not yet buried'. Naturally, this proverb is found amongst the votaries of Bawon Samedi and the Guédeh laws, because here we find the mercury that binds stars and death. Milo Rigaud associates the Guédeh with the planet Nébo—Mercury—because psychopomps and prophets they are. From this we can see a temperament revealed in their colour scale of black, white and purple. Purple is a colour made from a combination of blue and red, water and fire, being the mercurial snake road where the dead live and the living die. Purple is the colour of cardinals and bishops; it is a regal ray in the Church erected on the bones of St. Peter—the Bawon of the Vatican... So naturally, it is a colour rightfully belonging to Bawon Samedi, La Croix, Carrefour and so forth. Purple is the mystery of setting water aflame as the blood of lambs drips from the cup of Helios and gives life to the Bawon's bones. It is the colour of resurrection and transubstantiation—a mystery the Christian Church adopted from the practices of Greeks and Romans, where the dead were quickened by wine, water and bread. Some examples are the cakes and Haoma wine in the cult of Mithras that went through a mystical transformation foreshadowing the entire mystique of the Eucharist. Transubstantiation is a primitive doctrine, the sanctification of something ordinary into something otherworldly, like turning bread into flesh, water into wine and wine into blood. As such, the Guédeh are this mystery and Bawon Samedi is the cardinal presiding over it.

Upon death we can be forgotten and enter a state of forgetfulness as we cross the river Lethe. We can, by heroic deeds or by being loved by nymphs and daimons, become stars and starry constellations as we can ascend to the many halls of Tartaros, or the Elysian fields at the western part where the end of the Earth meets Tartaros in the equatorial river Oceanos. For the Greek *goes* there was a clear difference between the *nekudaimon,* or corpse daimon, and the *katachthonios daimon,* or underworld daimon—but they were located in the same realm albeit in different halls. We also know that many nymphs could walk freely between the invisible realm of Tartaros and the world of humans. If we add to these revenants and all forms of undead spirits and beings, we see that death is quite vibrant. Homer and Hesiod perceived the world as an egg where our plane of existence was conceived as a disk or globe in the centre of the egg. Earth would then be the prism that reflected both heaven and hell, the celestial and the chthonic. In other words, earth is the balance between heaven and hell.

Death is about perspective, and when the dead ascend to counsel, this is what they give. Necromancy is the *mantike,* or divinatory art of using the 'dead' to counsel us, to comfort us, to give revelation. Death is prophecy and thus Moses, Enoch, Ezekiel and Isaiah were necromancers in their capacity of prophecy by dream, vision or intoxication. As such, necromancy is simply the summoning and prophetic interrogation with the denizens in the Titanic realms of Tartaros, Oceanos and Hades.

Necromancy as a practice involves prayers, libation and there is often the air of Solomonic command at play in such workings. It has a distinct Saturnine flavour to it in its work with earth and all things chthonic, but rarely have the dimensions of water and woman been addressed in necromantic discourse and it is this dimension I will seek to comment upon in the following pages.

WATERS FROM THE ABYSS

Necromancy holds a markedly masculi6ne aura, but the mystery of necromancy is only possible by virtue of woman. Woman is the womb of miracle.

Woman can gestate seeds of light in the chaotic waters of the womb and bring forth life and in this replicate the dual mystery of hell and heaven—be it birth or rebirth. We see in the accounts of Hesiod and Homer the influence of Aphrodite in several accounts speaking of Tartaros and Hades and the communion with its denizens. Circe should also be mentioned as she was the one who gave necromantic secrets to Homer. Circe typifies the purple mystery incarnated by being the offspring of Helios, the Sun and the ocean-id Perse. She can, like a nymph, move freely between realms, and as such she walks the points of Mercury in the waters of hell as much as heaven. The turbulent waters of secrecy, the ocean of chaos that gave birth to dragons and the primordial race was represented by Tiamat and probably the enigmatic Tethys, foster mother of Hera and architect of the starry constellations.

The Guédeh are walking the points of Mercury. They are the shining host in the abysmal waters of the Great Dragon. This dragon water is the fabric of space, be it liquid or aerial, and manifests itself in 'houses of God'—woman. This mystery is exemplified in traditional Vodou by the relationship Bawon Samedi holds with the icon of St. Mary of Magdalene at the Sepulchre. Mary Magdalene weeping at the tomb represents the potency of transubstantiation; the tears shed in the absence of love holds the power of transmutation. These tears, this 'dragon water' from Tiamat's salty sea, is what resituates her beloved and brings her star to shine yet again in the celestial graveyard where heroes and lwa mark the constellations.

The waters are where we find death, ancestry and legacy. In our blood, the memory of how we became who we are flows through our heart as a constant reminder of this fact. The waters took on an even greater dimension in the Transatlantic crossing that brought the memory of so many Africans to the mysterious realm often called Calunga, the palace of Mami Wata at the bottom of the Ocean, which holds their legacy.

Necromancy is an art of water, and it rightly belongs to women as midwives and their capacity of gestating seeds in darkness to bring them to light. Fire is the paradoxical product of this mystical work with waters. Women, like Mary Magdalene or Myriam, sister of Moses, replicate the role of Naman Brijit in Vodou. They are the waters of recitation and resurrection, the nigromantic water and pulse of space, liquid and aerial.

By the use of magical waters we aim, through alchemical contrast, to bring fire to quicken our communion. In this, we replicate the abysmal order of death, return and becoming; because death and transition is truly intricate in the life of any star. Death is of the Earth, but when it gains motion by its fusion with water and generates mud, we find mercury, the element and spirit of psychopomps. Earth moves—and so does we—and in this Nature herself moves through stars and death.

Death is never the end; it is a transition and transformation, a homecoming of sorts. Like the Earth itself goes through cycles, mainly mirrored by seasons and natural phenomena, so do humans in their incarnations. In a similar fashion, the waters revel in the changes and give us rain, hail, fountains and geysers. Waters are, like earth, of a wide variety of qualities ranging from stale and lifeless to invigorating and golden. It is the motion of passions, like the Earth is the motion of memory. Waters are blood; it is the juice of herbs, the fiery waters from the alchemist's laboratory of distillation and the very medium that makes all forms of attraction possible.

The importance of waters in necromancy is exemplified by the various formulas of manufacturing sacred ink and oils—but also the formulae found in several grimoires where a human skull or head is taken and planted with black beans in the eye sockets. One example is found in the Bernardakean Magical Codex and replicated in the Grand Grimoire and Grimoire of Honorius, although with a distinctly different purpose, namely to catch shadows or to open a gate for communion. One of these formulas is given as follows:

At the 29th day of the Moon, at the hour of Mercury, take the head of a dead man or of a black cat that has not a single white hair. Then, take seven black chickpeas. Put one in the mouth, one in each ear, two in the nose—that is to say one in each nostril—and two in the eyes. After you have put them there, recite the following:

O you Hermes, most holy craftsman of invisibility, o you Hermes Mercury, Nagodiômêda, Theophilon, Person, Dôna, Neomêta, Prokorsou, I conjure you by God who created you to make this work of invisibility effective, in order for me to be invisible, unseen by all men, when I carry the seed.

Put it in a flowerpot and when you water it for the first time use human blood taken from phlebotomy. Take care of them until they yield seed. When they are dry, be careful not to lose any of the seeds.

The head should then be fed with waters of a variety of different properties to give birth to the ladder of hell so the dead can ascend. Because, truly, as Hermes Trismegistus told in his famous axiom: 'as above, so below'; if Angels can descend, the Dead can ascend.

The *Papyri Grecae Magicae* gives a host of similar spells using the heads of animals, but often these are workings done with the aid of the Sun and not with Mercury. This is no surprise seeing that solar deities like Shemesh, Orpheus, Apollo and Circe's father, Helios, held a distinct chthonic dimension in their ability of bringing the Sun to Tartaros. Hence the laurel wand, gold and the Sun is what tempts and controls this balance that enables necromancy.

In many cultures, we find stories, myths and legends of inhabitants of invisible realms, be they fairy, djinn or iwin that abduct the living to their sanctuary in the wood, the ocean or 'the other side'. A common theme is that the abducted is thought of as dead and time moves slower in the place of abduction, making their return a resurrection. To leave this world, this reality we living have agreed upon, is a death. It is transition and transformation.

With the Vodou mystés La Siren and Bawon Samedi, we find the paradox of how the living is brought to temporal death and how the dead become temporally alive, challenging our worldview and our materialistic ideas of reality, hinting towards a greater dynamic and a wider landscape of ingress and expansion.

La Siren, the mysté of seduction, poetry and music, is also the sorcerous powers of the Ocean. She is known to abduct babies and to bring sailors to a watery death. She is usually considered a Rada lwa—and this is true—but we need to understand that Rada is *rasin*, of the root, and not a reference to the 'calm' lwa of Vodoun. Rada is the royal side of Vodou, where the memory of *Ginen* and even memories more distant pulsate deeply within each of the lwa that find their place there. All of them have their fiery aspect and can turn *Petwo*, or *la flambeau* so to speak. La Siren turns *petwo* when she seeks death and threat, but then she is no longer La Siren, but Brijit, wife of Bawon Samedi, where she, like a shark, generates whirlpools in the waters to bring you down to her dark depths. This aspect of La Siren is found in the prime representation of Bawon Samedi, the cross. The cross holds in Vodou several secret meanings, and one of them is that the root of the cross stretches down in the abysmal waters where we find Brijit as an Undine Queen, a dragon. Hence together they are the perfect mercury of any psychopomp dancing in the waters abysmal and celestial and generate the possibility for ascent as much as for descent.

This motive is not unique to Vodou; rather we see here a traditional theme found in several cultures. I will therefore stretch this golden thread of waters to Scandinavia and Ireland in order to emphasise this particular theme.

RÁN AND THE ROAD OF MEAD

The jotun-woman Rán was said to have nine daughters manifesting in the storms and waves of the ocean; hence they represent her nine temperaments, which also replicates the register of La Siren through her mother Brijit. In Norse mythology we find the concept of *Ránar vegr*, the road of Rán, and in her road the shades of a necromantic theme can be perceived. Rán herself is associated with gold, so much that gold is often a kenning for her, and gold is the metal most favoured by the Sun. Skáldrskaparmál says:

Hrauð í himin upp glóðum	*to the sky shot up the Deep's Glades,*
hafs, gekk sær af afli.	*with fearful might the sea surged:*
Börð, hygg ek, at ský skerðu.	*methinks our stems the clouds cut,-*
Skaut Ránar vegr mána	*Rán's road to the moon soared upward.*

This passage is a poetic rendering from the saga of Harald Hårfagre, where we find the following written:

Ut á mar mætir	*the assailants on the teeth of the sea*
Mannsksædr lagar tanna	*dangerous to all men*
Ræsinadr til rausnar	*like a serpent upon the waters it was*
Rak vebrautar Nökkví.	*the vessel's stem making Nökkvís road*

Nökkví is the father of Nanna, wife of Balder, and daughter of the Moon. With Balder's death, wolves eat the Sun and Nanna, the Moon, dies of grief. By setting Balder's burial ship on fire, the couple is reunited in Hel. What is interesting here is that the roads of Rán and Nökkvi seem to be identical. The reference to the 'vessel's stem' is about the serpentine carvings given to the ships, a sign of concord and amity with Jormundgan and the dragon powers of the Ocean. Not only this, it was also a symbol for this particular road that stretched from the golden and mysterious depth of Rán to Nökkvi's ship, the moon. This ship was seen particularly in the waxing and waning phases of the moon whose shape in those junctures would give the idea of a ship. As we know from any traditional work with the moon, waxing moon and waning moon represents important phases of increase and decrease of whatever spell is under consideration. We also find Bragí, the patron of poets and troubadours to rest in Nökkví's ship and refresh himself with special mead from Jotunheim (the abode of Jotuns), the very same mead we find in the well of Mimir. This mead is old and made possible by the road of Nökkví—which is also Rán's road. Hence the Moon and the depth of the Ocean hold an uncanny relationship with Mimir, 'the remembrance of wisdom'.

It was this mead poets (*skaldr*/troubadours) drunk from—and it was also this mead that would cause the particular memory that would give *gandr* and *galdr* their power as it was also this mead of memory that revealed secrets. The snake road of Nökkví and Rán was also the veritable key for opening the mysteries of what was concealed—and this included death. This mead was golden, like the apples of Idun, like the secret held by Rán—the same secret that was found in the belly of Nökkví's ship.

So we find here a similar mystery playing itself out as we find in relation to Mary Magdalene at the Sepulchre, as we find in the dynamic between La Siren, Brijit and Bawon Samedi. It is here we find the *psychagogia* possible, to 'rise the dead'. It should be mentioned that the epitaph *gogia*, 'to lead', was commonly used in reference to erotic spells of love and binding, revealing a deep connection with the principles of erotic attraction to resuscitate the dead and make a road for their egress. This is perhaps most famously typified by Orpheus and Eurydice, which reveals that some form of erotic bond must be forged in a necromantic work. With 'erotic' I have in mind the classical idea that a functional vinculum must be forged by the aid of *eros* by giving attention to the mechanism of attraction in the bond forged. Naturally the tears of love and the blood of a broken heart can serve as a powerful bond, but there are also the waters of sorrow and despair as related to Brigid.

BRIGID AND THE TEARS AT EN-DOR

When we embark on necromantic work, what are we really working with? Are we resuscitating the dead, are we calling a memory floating in the ether or are we calling the attention of spirits of death? I believe the greater work of necromancy does traffic with all of these and also with spirits of the other side, fairies and telluric daimons of a great variety that have in common a concealed sublunary existence. The necromancer and the psychopomp, or guide of souls, are both working the points of Mercury. Mercury, being a fluid metal, is naturally represented by wines and water used for libations and medium for transmutation and also magical food for various ends, like the Witches' Sabbath wine that also works on the points of Mercury.

In the biblical books we find the account of the necromancer in the city of En-Dor. The account is spoken of in 1. Samuel 28: 8, 9 where we read:

> *Then said Saul unto his servants: 'Seek me a woman that divineth by a ghost, that I may go to her, and inquire of her.' And his servants said to him: 'Behold, there is a woman that divineth by a ghost at En-dor.'*
>
> *And Saul disguised himself, and put on other raiment, and went, he and two men with him, and they came to the woman by night; and he said: 'Divine unto me, I pray thee, by a ghost, and bring me up whomsoever I shall name unto thee.'*

We learn that the necromancer was in possession of an *ob*, a telasim/talisman. *Ob* can also be a reference to a wineskin, that it was a particular wine that was the charm itself. It might be that we see here a reference to a special mead, wine or water that would quicken the dead either by being used for anointing her as a medium for receiving the spirit, or as libation to generate the snake road of ascent for the spirit of Samuel. We see here a case of divination by *nekudaimon*, to resuscitate a corpse daimon. Prayerful lamentations made frequent part of these types of work in Antiquity, and it was often the role of women to lament in sorrowful weeping to gain the attention of the dead and other chthonic spirits. The importance of weeping—and its product, tears—is also found in the greater motive of Ireland's Brigid.

Brigid holds as her day the mass of candles on the first days of February, itself a liminial time, a waxing moon as it were, in the cycle of seasons. It is a glyph in time where light is given to the dead in the form of candles, food and drink. Brigid is known for her night travels and she is also credited with the origin of the Ogham oracle in her capacity as patroness of poets. Owls, serpents and bees belong to her as do doorways and thresholds—all totems worthy of a psychopomp and necromancer. She was also associated with wells and springs as well as fires—and from this she held a relationship with the intoxication of magical waters, like mead and beer. She also created the particular form of poetic mourning and weeping followed by the death of her son Ruadán, what is known as 'keening'. Keening serves the same function as the lamentation and songs used by the goes in Antiquity, speaking of her intimacy with the realm of the *nekudaimonos*.

The fair inhabitants of Annwn, the sidhe or banshee, are said to be inhabited by Brigid's soul. The sidhe could be summoned by the use of keening and were reputed to give prophecy and oracles—but also death... Brigid is, amongst many praise names, referred to as 'Lady of the Shores'. The shore is certainly represented by the Irish coastline—but also it refers to the shore separating the visible and invisible world. What we see here is a deep connection with female mysteries and the other side, something we also find in the concept of valkyrias.

This army of Odin, these misty 'daughters' of Freya that were not only guides of the soul on their way to Valhalla, but also those who elected who would be slain in battle and who would live. Odin held a particular affinity with them—but the valkyrias were in particular the providence of the Völva, given the fact that the Norns were in fact valkyrias. But then again, Odin was one of the few aesir who had submitted to the wisdom of women, something Loki gave him a hard time for in *Lokesenna*, which might explain why Odin was gifted with this army of valkyrias.

The valkyrias were also known for their connection with the drinking horns, the mead and games of chance and of particular importance should be mentioned the mead they prepared for Balder's funeral. The valkyrias were associated deeply with crows and bees and were said to rest in 'the airy sea', or mist. It follows that fairies, sidhe, norns, valkyrias and their intercessors—like the Völva and the votaries of Odin—were psychopomps and necromancers by disposition and could easily facilitate congress across realms.

We see a motive surface; a motive encoded in the icon of Mary Magdalene at the Sepulchre. Resting at the crossroad of death, flanked by crows, she allows honey to fall to the ground symbolized by her tears, and necromantic congress is effectuated by weeping and lamenting as she feeds the grave wine, water and bread. By virtue of her icon she exemplifies the simplicity involved in necromancy and the importance of the erotic bond and waters.

THE FOOD OF TOMBS

In works of necromancy we work with memories, and we do this through poetry, hymn and lamentation. It is intrinsic that a certain atmosphere is generated for the *psychagogia* to occur. Of the more direct strategies we find the laying down on the grave in question as candle, oil, wine, water and bread is fed to the departed as the departed is called by poetry, lament and ecstasy. This technique of embodying the dead is found in several faiths and is always regulated by a certain protocol. There is also the feeding of the grave by not laying down. In these cases a small fire could be made at the side of the grave, and the fire should then be fed 'death wood', like cypress and pine, and the ghost can be commanded or petitioned to use the smoke to shape its form. These modes involving fire and earth are by far more known than the path of waters; so therefore, I will give some formulas for working the dead by the use of waters. These workings, albeit simple, tend to give dramatic results, so I admonish to show care and good sense in the use of these waters. If you are an apprentice in these mysteries and have no idea about how to calm whatever rises from below, it is better to refrain.

WORKS WITH WATERS AND MIRRORS

Purple Water

One working I have found useful in order to forge a vehicle for spirits from the other side involves gathering water from a natural spring. You will to this water add leaves/flowers of laurel, orange, rosemary, datura stramonium and honeysuckle. These plant parts are macerated in the water when the Moon is in Cancer, in the night hour of Mercury. Cognac in sufficient amounts is added to the water in order to preserve it. It will then stay covered in darkness until the Moon is waxing or full in any sign ruled by Mercury (Gemini/Virgo). You will take this water to the location where you desire to have a communion with the dead, and you will pour the water over your naked body, cover yourself with a cotton cloth in white, black or purple and light a small fire. You will here in lamenting ways call up the spirit or deceased one while you give offerings of laurel to the fire—or you can fashion a lamp that you feed with laurel oil. You need to reserve some of the water and place it in a vessel of glass whereupon you place a glass fitting. The glass must be darkened or transparent but not a mirror, enabling you to 'see through'—but the darker it is the better. This vessel of glass covered with the mirror will then be placed in the point of power and used for scrying.

The prescribed water can also be used as a medium to dissolve planetary squares and produce a medium for communion with planetary intelligences. You will then in the appointed day and hour write out with dove's blood the square in question and charge the square with hymns and fumigations. The square will then be soaked in the water, and as the ink dissolves with

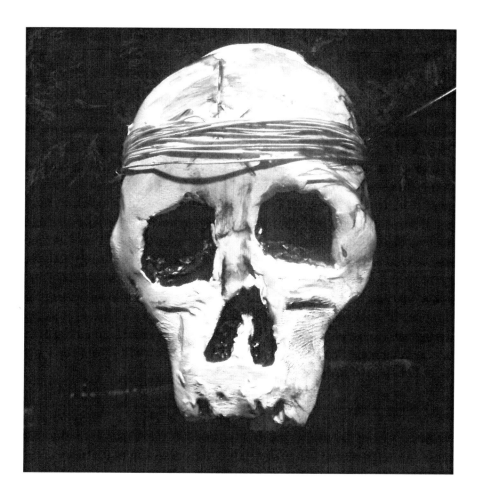

the water, it can be used for scrying, a body wash or libation to the planetary spirit, intelligence or genii in question.

Black Water

There is a 'black water' that can be made for necromantic summoning. This water should be made when the moon is waning towards its darkness. When the moon is in Aries, Scorpio, Leo or Capricorn is an auspicious time for the manufacturing of this 'black water'. You will use water from a spring or river, this being collected on a Tuesday in the hour of Mercury. To this water you will add laurel, leaves of nutty trees (for instance oak), holly, leaves of mandrake and leaves of mistletoe and dry white wine. Let the leaves stay in the water, covered with a black cloth until the appointed time. You will then bring the basin outside to be witnessed by the moon's vanishing light. You will add to the water gold dust and copper dust, and you will light coals around the basin. When the coals are red hot, they will be fed red wine, and while still glowing they will be added to the water. Let the water rest under the face of the moon for some hours, then take out the coals and the leaves and cover the water so no light will hit it. This water can then be used as charm for summoning the dead or chthonic spirits in the form of a libation given directly on the ground. This water can also be used as food for a bonfire, if one works with fire in the summoning, as much as it can be used as a body wash to facilitate possession with the summoned spirit. This water can also be used as drink for the dead where you pour the water directly on the grave, or to quicken bones buried in another place. If you seek to invigorate bones, you can take them to a place of power in nature and bury them. At this place libations of the water are given every night in the hour of Mercury during one lunar cycle and then dug up. This will produce a dreaming bone or a wishing bone. This bone needs to be fed regularly with the same water in order to keep it strong.

...AT THE END

Waters represent the field of the dragon, and it is the female mysteries that make this serpent road from the depth of the ocean and to the heart of the moon possible. This dragon road is found in how Bawon Samedi and Naman Brijit form a unity mirrored in the relationship Rán holds with Nökkvi and Odin with Freya that opens gates between all realms. This mead, this wine, this *ob* that forms this secret unity is a libation that quickens the dead, like blood quickens the body. Waters are of the Moon, but they walk the points of Mercury when agitated, and through these paths, roads and possibilities crooked and straight are made accessible.

From the waters come the sirens and nymphs of poetry. It was the waters that brought Orpheus' head to the island of Lesbos. And thus it was the road of Rán that was opened for the resuscitation of Orpheus' memory as he rode on the violence of Brijit and the sweetness of La Siren. And it is in this the memory we can resurrect with necromancy lies encoded. Water is a conductor and it is glass and mirror—that which gives the illusion of transparency is in reality earth in motion—and naturally together they form the cornerstone of any *mantike*, any attempt of crossing realms. The necromantic road is of waters and mirrors, while fire is food and ladder—and since fire is a ladder, the paradox of the importance of water often ends up in the shade of the mystery. In the presence of this mystery, it is easy to forget the 'fiery' quality of a turbulent ocean that moves in waves of foam as lightning strikes down to bring memory to the surface. Bawon Samedi and Naman Brijit is this mercurial turbulence on the Saturnine Ocean of the many souls and La Siren is the lunar poetry that causes this movement and veils the necromancer in the wines of Venus and Mercury as the invisible and visible world merges into a new landscape where the dead live and the living die...

NATHTANTRIKA PITRA PAKSHA PUJA
(HONORING THE ANCESTORS
& HALLOWED DEAD)

Hermeticusnath (Aion 131)

This Puja (devotional magickal ritual) is to honor the Dead. The godforms are traditional Tantric Deities but with the interesting exception that an ancient Vedic god, Agni, as the Living Flame, forms the gateway for the Dead so that they may come and commune with the living who honor them. We have performed this Puja at our Zonule with our Kula with amazing results. Last time, a lamp exploded and all of us perceived the honored dead about us in a circle just out of the bonfire's light. Shanti shanti shanti! Peace to the honored dead, gratitude for the blessings they give us. OM!

(This ritual will appear in a future book of rituals tentatively titled NATHTANTRIKA RITUALS)

OM GAM GANIPATYE NAMAH! x3 (offerings to Ganesh)
PHAT x5 BANISHING
Hands Held
Circle Cast:
SHANTI SHANTI SHANTI! x11

IN THIS TIME AND PLACE OF DARKNESS
AT THE CROSSROADS OF LIFE AND DEATH

AT THE PORTAL OF THE UNDERWORLD
LET US MEDITATE ON YAMA,
THE GOD OF DEATH,
THE BLACKNESS OF TRANSFORMATION
WHO HIDES THE INNER FLAME OF LIFE LOVE AND
LAUGHTER!
IGNITING IN THE PLACE OF DARKNESS
LET US CALL FORTH THE LIGHT BEYOND LIGHT
SO THAT WE MAY BLESS AND PETITION
THE HONORED DEAD.
OM...

OM VAISVANARAYA VIDHMAHE LALELAYA DHIMAHI
TANNO AGNIH PRACHODAYAT x3 (fire lit)

As a lens of crystal we magnify the divine Light Agni, the primal fire of Creation itself, we call forth the portal of sacrifice and fountain of blessings and treasure!

Agni! God of fire and power and Light be magnified now through the lens of the Great Teachers and open the way for the Gods to bless this Puja and all Present!

Agni! Bring health, wealth, prosperity and Liberation to the Great Teacher, Our Beloved Dead and to all beings, including to this Kaula Circle! Bring Bliss, Bring Joy, bring Victory!!

All we offer to you O Agni is given into the arms of the Gods – bring the Divine Blessings forth to empower and honor this Puja!

Agni, great Patron of the Tantrika. Giver of Bliss; you who are at every ritual and who are Truth, come be here now; and with you the Gods.

Fill us with the Great Work, let the divine Work through us that the Greatest Work of all may manifest – we all burn with the flame of Agni!

You are the sunlight, you shine at night within the darkness – You are the Energy God, the God of Transformation and Guardian of the sacred Flaming Goddess of Love!

Always come easily Agni, you are welcome here

May we be as your children, as small flames sparked by a massive flame

For we are all Stars!

OFFERINGS TO THE FIRE:
OM DEVAN TARPAYAMI NAMAH! x3
Bless us and bless our work O AGNI STARFIRE !
May all we do
Honor the Gods, the Teachers and the Ancestors/Friends
May all we say and do
Generate merit for them
and for all sentient beings.
OM!
OM NAMO AGNI RUPAAYA MAMA SHARIRE
STAMBHAN KURU KURU SVAHA ! x3
Bless us and bless our work O MAHADEVA!
May all we do
Honor the Gods, the Teachers and the Ancestors/Friends
May all we say and do
Generate merit for them
and for all sentient beings.
OM!
OM NAMAH SHIVAYA! x3
Bless us and bless our work O MAHADEVI!
May all we do
Honor the Gods, the Teachers and the Ancestors/Friends
May all we say and do
Generate merit for them
and for all sentient beings.
OM!
HRIM SRIM KRIM PAREMESHVARI SVAHA! x3

MAY WE BE BLESSED AND PURIFIED BEFORE THE
GOD AND GODDESS, MAY ALL SHADOWS MELT
AWAY, MAY THE LIGHT FILL AND NOURISH US THAT
WE MAY HONOR THE BLESSED DEAD.
(Bless the three body centers with smoke from the offering fire)
OM SHANTI SHIVA SHAKTI x3
CHARGE AND BLESS THE SACRED WATER (TARPAN)
–all extend hands and pour the blessings into the water

– added to the Tarpan are Milk (water), honey (fire), grain (earth), flower petals (air), ghee (spirit)

All chant:
OM MANI PADME HUM x108

OFFERINGS TO THE NORTH:
OM SHI GURU PADUKKUM PUJAYAMI TARPAYAMI
NAMAH SVAHA
OM SHRI SANTA SHRI GURDEV MAHENDRANATH
OM NAMASTE TO THE CRYSTAL LINE OF NATH GURUS!
WE GIVE OFFERINGS OF JOY AND PEACE TO THE
GREAT TEACHERS THE HONORED WISEMEN AND
WOMEN WHO ARE NOW SPIRIT
THOSE OF WISDOM AND POWER AND STRENGTH WE
HONOR YOU
NAMASTE!

Each goes to the NORTH and offers Tarpan (sacred water) to his/her TEACHERS and to all of the Honored Gurus, Helpers and Guides.

All chanting OM SHANTI SHANTI SHANTI!

OM PITRUS TARPAYAMI NAMAH!
WE GIVE OFFERINGS OF JOY AND PEACE TO THE
ANCESTORS
FROM TIME BEYOND TIME, WE OFFER TO OUR
BLOOD, OUR BONES, OUR FLESH
THE GOLDEN THREAD OF DNA AND ALL WHO HAVE
GIVEN US EVERYTHING
THE SILVER THREAD OF LOVE AND FRIENDSHIP OF
THE EXTENDED CIRCLE
THANK YOU AND BLESS YOU!
WE ASK THAT YOU HONOR AND BLESS US
LOVED ONES AND FOREFATHERS AND FOREMOTHERS
WHO ARE NOW SPIRIT

*THOSE WHO WE REMEMBER, THOSE WHO ARE
FORGOTTEN BUT ABIBE, WE OFFER TO YOU AND
ASK THAT YOU HELP US IN OUR WAY AND WILL,
WITH LOVE
NAMASTE!
SESEME SEEDS ARE ADDED TO THE TARPAN WATER…*

Each goes to the SOUTH and offers Tarpan (sacred water) to his/her loved dead, ancestors and friends…

All chanting OM SHANTI SHANTI SHANTI!

*RETURN TO WESTERN (Mail) ALTAR – FINAL PRAYERS
IN SILENCE
OFFER TO FIRE
All burn candles to their honored dead–*

*ASATO-MAA, SAD GAMAYA x3
– From untruth to Truth!
TAMASOMA, JYOTIR GAMAYA 3X
– There lies the light of wisdom.
MRITYOR MAA, AMRITAM GAMAYAA 3X
– Lead me from death to (true will).*

*OM SHANTI, SHANTI, SHANTI
– Let there be peace in 3 worlds
SVECCHACHARA!
FINAL BOW:
THANK YOU O HONORED GODS, TEACHERS AND
ANCESTORS/FRIENDS
RETURN NOW TO THE OTHER SIDE BUT BLESS AND
GUIDE US AS WE NEED
HELP US WITH KNOWLEDGE, THE TRUTH OF WILL
AND BALANCED ACTION
NAMASTE! AND FAREWELL– Svaha!*

*HEALTH WEALTH PROSPERITY AND LIBERATION TO
ALL BEINGS!
MAY ALL BEINGS FIND PEACE!
OM SHANTI SHIVA SHAKTI x3
PHAT x5   (ALL WATER LEFT OFFERED TO A TREE)*
(Other offerings to the fire at will – all earthed…)

THE LAST TOUCH OF THE GREAT POISONER

Ljóssál Loðursson

Throughout the centuries the power of life and death has been one of the most coveted treasures by magicians, occultists, mystics, nigromancers and necromancers. Some seek to destroy the diseases that weaken the body by concentrating their forces in physical practices and forms of power that give them longevity; some even try to develop mythical siddhis such as immortality of the body. Others seek more effective methods such as sowing death and destruction to annihilate their enemies and take control over the life force of the universe around them. In both cases the development of such skills involves a complete dedication to the Royal Art in order to obtain a result that can be truly effective; health or sickness, *"sanatio-aut ægrotatio"* as Roman doctors would say, is a process of capacity, skill, knowledge and possibly of personal vocation.

In these years of practice in the art, I have experienced how the flow of life energy that is within and around us is constantly internalized, altered or transformed. Hindu and Nordic schools agree that the core of this life force is found in the breath and the action of breathing. Prana or Önd is absorbed by each individual and is the bridge between the physical body and the astral body; in the moment when the last breath is issued these two bodies become separated and the Journey to the otherworld begins. There are various modern and ancient grimoires which provide specific techniques that can interfere with the flow of vital energy from other beings and affect their health or any aspect of their lives. These processes are methods of evocation, ritual curse spells or sympathetic magic that represents the death of the victim.

Many practitioners become frustrated when trying to destroy their enemies, trying to make their enemies gasp their last breath but realizing that despite their efforts they are still alive. Part of this frustration happens because the result has not appeared in the expected time or the disease has not reached the desired intensity. To permeate this situation and improve all skills related to the destruction and ruin of our adversaries we must integrate an adequate consciousness capacity related to this work. This is what I call the Last Touch of the Great Poisoner.

ENTHRONIZE

The first step is to invoke or enthrone the forces of death in ourselves, many practitioners fail in their rituals of destruction because they do not understand the natural cycle of life and death; they hope to control a force which they are unfamiliar with. I consider this similar to playing doctor without knowing the anatomy of the human body. To further this process the Black Arts practitioner must link his consciousness and will with any intelligence or spiritual force that rules over death and the dead, destruction and disease; Dark Father Qayin or the Mother of the Tree of Death Hella are an excellent example of this. Each initiate must find, regardless of their tradition, a dark divinity which may favor him in this work. This is an intuitive process, almost instinctive and must be under all standards a personal choice and not instilled by someone else. Once we found that Tutelary Deity, we must delve into the Underworld to familiarize ourselves with his energy. This process is akin to traveling to the Underworld enunciated by the Greeks as Katabasis and by the Norse as Helwegr, a journey where our consciousness, will and soul go through a dangerous but empowering road. The practice should align the three subtle bodies beyond the physical body and align them with the forces of transmutation and death so that our being can be able to integrate the best knowledge and energies of the Chthonic realms.

The Enthronement occurs by performing various ceremonies or devotional practices to our Tutelary Deity in order to receive information and delve into its mysteries. We investigate which offerings are pleasing to our deity, his prayers and songs, rubrics, sigils or seals inhabited by his magic. The words of power, called mantras or galdr, influence on us, and we can make some Japas on their behalf to attract their presence. Some deities have a particular day on which may be called or held; Tantric Pujas and Nordic Blót exemplify this. We perform acts of sincere devotion and surrender to generate a deep spiritual bond with that power. This practice has a gradual development and is something that takes time; the wise Black Arts practitioners understand that good crops are given after a good time of harvesting. Each journey to the Underworld should be initiated during a New Moon/Dark Moon.

Itineris Carnis – Journey of the Flesh

The first trip to the underworld will awaken in us the blessing of our mortuary deity in the astral body. To make this first trip we follow a 9 consecutive day process in which we give a constant devotional process towards our personal Chthonic teacher. The number 9 represents death as such because it is the end of single digits, the 3 x 3 of the Valknutr, the nine realms of Heldrasil or the 9 roads of the Mexican Xibalba. Every day we light incense in our altar, take a moment to make invocations or calls, sing words of power, light candles or leave offerings marked with the name of our deity and anointed with oils or essences. At this stage we must use a magical tool to accompany us throughout the journey. It can be a Japamala with which we make our calls or a talisman to attract the necromantic power of our teacher. This tool will be the energy receptacle of the journey of the flesh. As our Astral body will be the first recipient to receive the wisdom of this journey, it is common to perceive dreams, daydreams or private trance states in which we will receive the mysteries of this first phase of the Underworld; here we depend on our flesh, and we have to hear the voices of the spirits.

Itineris Sanguinis – Journey of the Blood

The second trip to the underworld awakens in us the blessing of our mortuary deity in the mental body. The second journey is a little heavier as it involves the same devotional process for a period of nine weeks. The journey becomes more extensive. Something that is critical is that we must not stop under any rule, no matter how simple the daily practice this should not be suspended; we must nurture the bond with the chthonic kingdoms and respect the journey to the Underworld. The journey of blood shows us mental images, whispers, voices, intuitions or visions. These mysteries are transmitted in the second phase. In the journey of blood we use a wand, a knife or a sickle as a tool with which we draw sigils in the air of our Deity during celebrations or evocation and invocation acts. I have seen some magicians abandon the process at this point because when they establish the link with the realm of the dead it is common to lose loved ones, from pets to family; they have lost important relationships in their lives, many do not understand that their Tutelary Deity is leading them through an isolation process in order to temper his spirit. The loss of these factors is a form of personal transmutation or internal alchemy which seeks to teach the traveler which implies the transience of the world around us. This is the mystery of the Blood, the severance of ties and chains that bind us to the earth.

Itineris Osseum – Journey of the Bones

The third trip to the underworld awakens the blessing of our mortuary deity in the spiritual body. The third trip is the longest of all and not many are able to complete it due to its depth and temporal extent. You need 9 lunar months, 9 x 28 days. As in previous trips we make the same daily devotional process, but now we will give to our necromantic teacher a seat in our personal universe. To do this we make a special ceremony during each New Moon or Dark Moon during these nine lunar months. In this ceremony we must try to internalize and invoke the full force of the Deity. In these practices we can use plants or drinks that will lead to a liminal trance in which we perceive that the breath of life that holds the Subtle Bodies seems to weaken. The use of tobacco, wormwood, ayahuasca or any agent that induces a Thanatopathia status is valid here. Each Dark Moon powerfully tunes the awareness of the individual to receive the most profound teachings about the process of death; each Dark Moon is sustaining his will and thus strengthening his energy or personal power. During this trip it is possible to have or perceive direct experiences related to death, the dead and the renewal of cycles, funerals, accidents, terminal illnesses, births or drought. The process may occur more outwardly than the two previous trips. Our teacher prepares us to confront the daily death and rebirth, internally and externally. This is the experience of teaching that gets implanted in our bones. During this phase we will use a receptacle as a tool for our Tutelary Deity, a statue or effigy made with our own hands or established by ourselves. The statue must always remain in our altar or sacred space, and we use the nine months of the journey to build it. The last day of the Journey of the Bones, we perform a special thanksgiving ceremony to our guide and offer some of our blood, saliva and sexual fluids as a symbol of everlasting union with it.

Having finished the three journeys we will have completed the process of Enthronement and will now have a deeper understanding about death and transmutation states. With this we now have a basic praxis to get into the practices of curse, destruction and fatal magic.

Something interesting to notice is the ratio number of the three journeys to the Enthronement:

Journey of the Flesh: 9 days
Journey of Blood: 9 weeks, 9 x 7 = 63 days (6 + 3 = 9)
Journey of the Bones: 9 x 28 = 252 days (2 + 5 + 2 = 9)

9 + 63 + 252 = 324.
3 + 2 + 4 = 9

The cycle is closed as the Black Dragon devours itself; the Alpha and the Omega merge into one.

A word of advice: if we fail in one journey and not continue with the process, we must repeat the journey in which we find ourselves. It is very important to be honest with ourselves and not to try to take shortcuts in this path; the anxiety payment when transiting through the realm of death is usually quite high—let us remember Orpheus and Eurydice. Another factor is that the time interval between journeys cannot exceed 63 days, roughly two months. If we go over two months, it is advised to start over.

CHANNELING

The practitioner is now an avatar of death, a dedicated necromancer. The forces of Mars and Saturn dwell therein and understand the notion of cycles. He is now a container where the alchemical iron and lead of the Sinister Path and the Dark way constantly and incessantly converge. The mind's eye is now able to understand the flow of mortuary energies; it may easily perceive the line between the world of the living and the dead. We now turn to the process that involved causing death. According to Buddhist necromantic wisdom, the death process is based on the dissolution of the elements. As humans we consist of the four elements of nature. When we are dying, each element leaves the physical body independently and gradually contributing to the weakening of the body. Once all the elements leave the physical body, we enter the Underworld. From an ancient Tibetan medical text:

> *"The consciousness of the senses comes from the mind. The flesh, bones, the organ of smell and odors create from the Earth Element. The blood, the organ of taste, flavor and body*

fluids emerge from the Water Element. Heat, light color, the organ of sight and form come from the Fire Element. The breath, the organ of touch and physical sensations arise from the Air Element. The cavities of the body, the organ of hearing and sounds are formed from the Space Element."[1]

Another interpretation of this process is explained by Sogyal Rimpoche in *The Tibetan Book of Living and Dying:*

Earth
Our body begins to lose all its strength. We are drained of any energy. We cannot get up, stay upright, or hold anything. We can no longer support our head. We feel heavy and uncomfortable in any position. Our complexion fades and a pallor sets in. Our cheeks sink, and dark stains appear on our teeth. It becomes harder to open and close our eyes .These are signs that the earth element is withdrawing into the water element.

Water
We begin to lose control of our bodily fluids. Our nose begins to run, and we dribble. There can be a discharge from the eyes, and maybe we become incontinent. We cannot move our tongue. Our eyes start to feel dry in their sockets. Our lips are drawn and bloodless, and our mouth and throat sticky and clogged. The nostrils cave in, and we become very thirsty. We tremble and twitch. The water element is dissolving into fire.

Fire
Our mouth and nose dry up completely. All the warmth of our body begins to seep away, usually from the feet and hands toward the heart. Our breath is cold as it passes through our mouth and nose. No longer can we drink or digest anything. We cannot remember the names of our family or friends, or even recognize who they are. The fire element is dissolving into Air

---

[1] *The Ambrosia of Heart Tantra*, commented and translated by the Dr. Yeshi Dhondhen and JhampaKelsang, Library of Tibetan Works and Archives, Dharamsala, 1977.

Air

It becomes harder and harder to breathe. The air seems to be escaping through our throat. We begin to rasp and pant. Our in breaths become short and labored, and our outbreaths become longer. Our eyes roll upward, and we are totally immobile. The mind becomes bewildered, unaware of the outside world. We begin to hallucinate and have visions. What is happening is that the air element is dissolving into consciousness. The winds have all united in the "life supporting wind" in the heart.

In this way we get to the last breath and begin our personal Helwegr or Katabasis. For the Necromancer it is very important to understand this process because when he chooses to focus a victim on his mind's eye, he needs to understand that the Last Touch of the Great Poisoner must re-create the same conditions or characteristics; the solution is a form of poisoning. To this end, we investigate certain aspects of nature that will serve as capacitors of Martial-Saturnine energy for this purpose. Each of these aspects should be added to rituals of aggression, curse or damnation to accelerate the process of dissolution of the elements in the victim:

CHANNELING THE EARTH

To accelerate the dissolution of the Earth Element, we can use within our operations bone powder obtained from three separate beings: powdered bone of a human, a bird and a black dog. The powder should be prepared and/or consecrated on a Saturday in the hour of Saturn or at a time when the Dark Sun is regent in Saturn. The powder is used to fill or cover dolls of sympathetic magic rituals. It can also be used to cover the edge of swords, daggers, axes or spears that are dedicated to magic, and these will be used in rituals of aggression. The dust is the garment of the dead body.

CHANNELING THE WATER

To accelerate the dissolution of the Water Element, we should prepare herbal incense with poisonous plants or plants with thorns, no matter the family of the same; it can be foliar, cauline or radicular. The elemental agents of the acacia, blackthorn, hawthorn, rose or cactus are excellent in this work. Dry these plants away from the light of the sun even if it takes several weeks to accomplish this. In the day and hour of the moon, grind and consecrate the plants, mix them with the thorns of the same, then store in a red bag or container and under no circumstance allow sunlight or profane hand touch again. Burning this incense on the coals calls the spirits of aversion and disease, spectral and vampiric entities that consume and prey on the life force of the victim. The incense is associated with the digging of the grave of the dead.

CHANNELING THE FIRE

To accelerate the dissolution of the Fire Element, we must prepare the anointing oil on the day and hour of Mars develop and/or consecrate an oil based in Mandrake, Nettle and Dragon's Blood (Croton Lechleri) and put inside it two small stone , an amethyst and an obsidian. Also put Runic Sigils or destruction, summoning seals of the spirits of disturbance, insanity and suffering. Use the oil to cover the victim's objects (pictures, figurines, clothing, etc.) During the ritual of aggression, this creates a direct link with the forces that infuse dementia, insanity and paranoia.

CHANNELING THE AIR

To accelerate the dissolution of the Air Element, we must prepare an *Asphyxiant Bottle* in the day and hour of Mercury. Dedicate a dark bottle; it can be green, red or black (if you want you can paint it). The bottle should have a wide opening, enough for it to store all the links that have been used to attack the victim, statuettes, sigils, clothes, rings, etc. The outside of the bottle should be covered with sigils and runes of death and annihilation. The bottle is used as we approach the end of the ritual of destruction; there we conjure the breath of the victim, we ask our Tutelary deity to capture the breath of our enemy in the bottle thereby capturing the essence of his life, then by our own power and will we decree the same so the conjunction between God and Mage Guardian directs the manifestation of the energy into this plane. Finally the bottle is closed with black candle wax and is then buried or stored in places where death is pronounced, a site where a murder or a suicide has occurred or a cemetery.

We must rely on our own power and leave the spell in our oblivion, in the depths of our memory and our being, so it can germinate in our unconscious, our inner Underworld. Only then can the spell really become powerful. If we keep expecting a result, it will not happen; this is identical to the process with sigils.

To give closure to these issues, it is important to clarify the Enthronement and channeling are equally important. We must not believe that we know or we dominate all; the relationship with the forces of death is something that involves one or several lifetimes of study and understanding. Do not skip any of these two foundations.

About Death

As I said before, many magicians or necromancers become frustrated when their enemy is not dead as expected; however, in my experience with Heleikin (Nordic Necromancy) and Ráðafeikin (Nordic Curses) I have learned that there are different types of death, and these are directly linked or connected to the dissolution of the elements explained by Tibetan Buddhist necromancy. In some cases the Underworld energies guided by our Tutelary Deity only "encroach" or "mutilate" one of the four elements of our victim, so our enemy experiences a kind of "zombie" dead or alive state when he is deprived of a particular item. Be consistent with your magic and examine in depth what has happened to your enemy in a reasonable time after the ritual. Carefully observe which of the four forms of death appeared, and observe how the poison has expressed itself; this leaves important clues about the root of your psychic and magical abilities:

Death by Air
The magical assault victim loses all its allies and friends, his words tumble against all truth and nobody trusts him, dark and damaging secrets come to light, people that loved him before now betray him, doors close to all social and communication factors or the environment seriously collapses and destroys his credibility in his personal universe. Spiritual Body damage.

Death by Fire
The victim of the attack has deep psychic internal changes; it awakens a powerful sense of guilt and bends his will. He becomes docile before us. He who at one time was our enemy now seeks to be our ally—we have so profoundly influenced in his being that we develop in him a need or urgency to approach us. Other symptoms of death through fire involve memory loss or the entry into a process of internal or mental confusion, the victim loses his

life objectives and feels alienated in everything he does, he loses his self-confidence and ends up leaving all his personal projects aside, and nothing generates pleasure or joy; the fire inside him has died. Mental Body damage.

Death by Water
The victim goes into deep states of depression or anxiety, loses track of reality and madness or dementia begin to move him, panic attacks, night terrors and unconscious fears arise powerfully to take control of his mind. If the victim enters altered states of consciousness, it results in out of control states full of anxiety and paranoia. In many ways this can be one of the worst deaths for a magician or practitioner of the art as Gnosis states are vital for his development. When this happens, the rival magician experiences his trances as heavy and ineffective, entities or spirits that used to help him are now leaving or attacking him since he has lost the power to dominate them. Astral Body damage.

Death by Earth
The death that is always desired and sought by all magicians or necromancers. In this type of operation there are accidents, an already acquired illness

severely worsens or develops in short periods of time, and all physical paths close to the victim except one, that leading to the tomb. This is the complete annihilation of the enemy.

You will notice that when death comes naturally the dissolution of the elements occurs in a specific order, from the most gross to the most subtle, from the earth to the air. However, when death occurs with a spiritual or magical influence the process becomes against nature; it dissolves from the most subtle to the most gross, from air to Earth. Understanding one model that can connect and direct the forces of death leads us to reflect on what poison we seek to prepare; thereby we become more accurate in the practice of the Black Art.

Mors super Vita!
Death over Life!

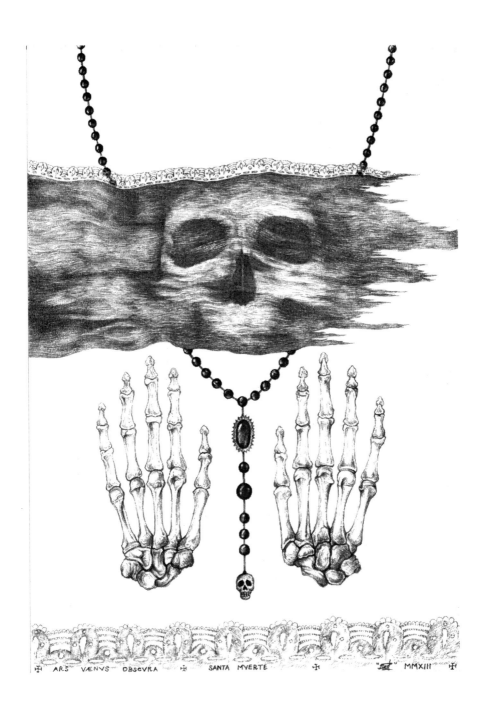

✠ ARS VENVS OBSCVRA ✠ SANTA MVERTE ✠ "𝓪𝓻𝓽" MMXIII ✠

THE CROWN OF BLACK THORNS: EXPLORATIONS AND INVOCATIONS OF OUR HOLY MOTHER DEATH

Edgar Kerval

T he purpose of this essay is to show in a clear and deep manner the foundations and principles of the worship of La Santisima Muerte, from an anthropological level, psychological and ritualistic. Also I have the pleasure to include three rituals from my experiences working with La Santisima Muerte months ago. We reveal the sacred mysteries of La Santisima Muerte, its rituals, traditions, and how it has been entering within the contemporary occult movement, as a strong current, which reaches imaginable limits.

We can feel the inner need to get into their most hidden mysteries, profound and sacred fruit thereof, after entering eternal gnosis that allows us to move into their roots and become one with them, penetrating the dark gnosis and taking the path of black alchemy to enlighten us with his black magic essence. The history of Holy Death or La Santisima Muerte comes from pre-Hispanic times, with the worship of gods and deities of Aztec culture. Here in South America as part of Central America, we found a great devotion-related death cult mother wing. Mostly in deeper regions of Paraguay and Argentina, as well as in some regions of Brazil and Colombia.

Some regions began to venerate La Santisima Muerte, worshiping bones or skeletons of ancestors to whom they prayed for protection against evil spirits. In parts of Brazil people worshiped the Santisima Muerte as a purely astral deity as an Exu in Quimbanda tradition. This is the case of a deity known as Exu Tata Caveira showing a close connection with the cult of La Santisima Muerte; we can also see a great devotion in Mexico especially in Central America with an annual celebration of Holy Death and the Dominican Republic and Haiti.

Although his practice has expanded to other regions, not only in Central America but in South America, such as Colombia, Venezuela, Ecuador, it has done so in a very limited way. Here, Pre-Hispanic animism connected with saints of Catholicism to the old aspect which was operated under a style of Cuban Santeria, which combines animism with Catholicism to African tradition. In this tradition some offerings were given to the lord of the death, the black cross lord, or holy mother death in different traditions.

Mictlantecuhtly and Mictecacihuatl were very important Aztec deities who were raised by all those who wished to connect themselves with the energy called death, and to possess the power of death. One of the most major temples of worship to these gods of death were found in Mexico City of Tenochititlan. Mictlantecuhtli is the god of death, lord of Mictlan, the quiet, dark realm of the dead. This Pre-Hispanic divinity is compared to Mayan god Duch Ah. This one was represented as a decaying body with a cadaverous head adorned with bells and necklaces of bones and feathers. Mictlantecuhtli was represented as a skeleton, or at least his head was a skull. The Aztecs, in order to placate Mictlantecuhtli, sent him lavish gifts, among which there were plenty of men's flayed skins to cover their bare bones.

The shape of death represents a very important element in our consciousness due its strong archetypical nature latent in us at every moment in our lives. This can be regarded in a kind of apprehension by certain individual, of acausal energies. Creates a psychic process which transcends into astral realms, creative artistic manifestations. Such fundamental principles relating death as an archetype lives in our psyche all the time and came out though some of our actions as thoughts, visions or expressive manifestations. Describing it, we can see for example the black robe used by the archetype of death, representing the way in which we hide our true appearance, behind another one. So as the black robe covering the skeleton which represents death itself, in the same way we hide ourselves in our flesh, out most in deep human nature which we masked in so many ways. Under this point we must observe how death's archetype is a living aspect in each one of us.

At the same point the scythe, the instrument of farming, represents the cycle of physical life which ends and the beginning of another existence, but this time not in the physical plane. The scythe shows us the equilibrium and balance which represents death as it is.

Also, the black color from holy death helps us to balance in the physical plane in all spheres we need to work with, and also gives us protection and helps in astral planes. The purple one helps us to enforce the psychic aspects, to move us in a secure way inside the spiritual worlds. It is known that red and black are colors related to darkness and the ritual works within the realms of the dead, necromancy.

DEATH ROSARY

By own experience, one of the most potent and strong magickal artifacts to connect with the essence or energy of La Santisima Muerte is the magickal use of death rosary. Each bean connected us with a powerful and magickal aspect of La Santisima Muerte. This magickal artifact must be built from wood, seeds or even bones or clay, just to name some of material properly used to build this. The principal point is that the sorcerer makes him/herself the construction of this, and to proceed to its consecration through each one of the rituals presented here.

The principal idea with the magickal rosary's construction is to include 59 beans, 50 black beans and 9 red beans. 5+9 =14; 1+4=5. Through this simple numerical operation we observe the dissolution of all beans (14; 1 [the magus] +4 [Portals of death]).The Physical Death, The Astral Death, The Spiritual Death, The Psychic Death. Into 5 the quintessence of man entering the realms of death, knowing that death is the gate of life, and this the most strong light, must be found in the most deep abyss which inhabits in the black shadow, in the pale face and spectral nature of our holy mother death.

So for construction of the magickal rosary, we must include 5 beans each day and work with ritual mantras and devotional prayers in front a statue of La Santisma Muerte with a black candle burning while we are including beans. As we mentioned before, red and black are colors of the beans, and such colors are related to darkness and the realms of the dead and necromantic works and the powerful connections into its hidden mysteries and its nature which is dark, wild and raw. Through magickal rosary we create a strong union to the psychic-spiritual level between sorcerer and the essence of the black flame of La Santisima Muerte.

The works with the magickal rosary can change according to many aspects from needs of the sorcerer. By our own experience we could work to curse or to destroy an enemy; for health works to increase vigorous and proper physical state, to you or someone you want to help; to spiritual works to gain access mysterious hidden knowledge; astral works to opening inner portals for connecting with the realms of dead; and divination works to gain access to worlds of perception and intuition to use in divination and connect this works within runes, tarot cards, crystals and other devices for divination.

CONSECRATION RITUAL

For consecration of our magickal rosary we must first have our proper ritual chamber or private place dedicated to La Santisima Muerte, a small room or room's corner with walls painted in black, a purple roof, and a proper wood table at side where the sun shows its last rays (East). This represents the fall of light and rebirth of darkness and kingdom of the night.

So connecting with the force of La Santisima is a state in which the sorcerer annihilates completely his/her own human personality and assumes an extreme state of dark psychic opening. He becomes completely open and receptive to the influx of energy and essence of La Santisima Muerte, which is an intense, intuitive and Tran-sensorial state of self-perfection and realization of an own reality in its fundamental and last aspect. To get connected with the essence of La Santisima, we are doing a conjunction of strong elements from our psyche which is the vacuity of senses and dissolution of matter in the hands of death itself. It is a rebirth with all its psychological, spiritual, and mental transformations beyond duality, beyond apparent reality of how we perceive things in this existential plane.

Implements:
- A Black Candle
- Death Rosary
- Black Box

The principal point with this elaborated ritual is to consecrate the magickal rosary, to influx this with the enigmatic essence of La Santisima Muerte in order to create a magickal artifact for the connection with her and dead spirits in a determinate magickal work. Before beginning with this ritual, it is of high importance to meditate for 7 days at sunset on a sigil of La Santisima Muerte which must be created especially for you and charged with your own blood.

To consecrate your death rosary, you must first get obsessed as most as you can of such essence, looking images of mother death, painting images, listening music, so everything which you can feel will be appropriate to cause a exhaustion of senses in all levels; the idea is to penetrate your unconscious realms with such atavist presence of La Santisima Muerte in all its mysterious splendor for you to carve and explore all facets surrounding its ancestral shape, with adorations, prayers, mantras, visuals, music, etc...

After meditating for 7 days at sunset, you must consecrate your death rosary for 7 days, doing 3 prayers each night at different hours. So let's begin with the ritual with the following steps. At first just keep your death rosary well hidden in a black box together with 5 small bones—the small bones represent here the essence of La Santisima in the physical plane. We use 5 bones because this represents the 4 elements in nature and the sorcerer as a fifth element. Burn the black candle, and before opening the black box to get the death rosary you must do the follow prayer to La Santisima in order get the necessary powerful energy to consecrate it.

> Prayer:
> *I invoke you goddess from death and darkness*
> *Spectral queen from the great void,*
> *Give me the powers to consecrate this death rosary in your name*
> *Unveiled one, show me your secret eye oh crowned queen of darkness*
> *Oh you, veiled one, give strong, give power, give me death*
> *Through this black flame and bones manifest in this artifact (death rosary)*
> *Incarnate your essence through this ineffable flame*
> *Ave muerte, Ave Santísima, Ave muerte*
> *Come, come come!!!*

Remember, you must do this invocation for 7 nights at sunset. Then open the black box and hold your death rosary in your left hand and let's pass it around the black candle's flame and repeat slowly:

> *Salve Mother Death*
> *Ave Santisima Muerte*
> *Hail crowned queen of darkness*
> *Through this black flame, give your powers*

To this magickal tool!!! Poison this with
Your infinite wisdom queen of the void
Salve Mother Death
Ave Santisima Muerte
Hail crowned queen of darkness

Visualize how a black spectral light comes from the fetish or statue of La Santisima to the black candle and from there though the death rosary. Then, let's put it around your neck and repeat:

Salve Mother Death
Ave Santisima Muerte
Hail crowned queen of darkness

And then, let's remove it from your neck, put it on the neck of the La Santisima Muerte fetish/statue and give thanks to her for all. For 7 days do the ritual exactly as it's explained here. After such period of time, keep the death rosary inside the black box at the altar and don't open it after a period of 7 days. After this time, you can use it when needed and can leave it around the neck of the La Santimima Muerte statue/fetish.

RITUAL TO GET ACCESS TO DEAD KNOWLEDGE

This powerful ritual is used to get hidden knowledge and secret symbols, sigils of the realm of the dead to use on diverse practices when invoking La Santisima Muerte.

Implements:
- La Santisima Muerte (fetish, statue)
- Death rosary,
- Quartz crystal.

With the coming sunset (6.00 p.m.), you shall enter to the cemetery fields and prepare a small altar at the east side. Including the statue or fetish of La Santismima Muerte. The magickal rosary must be put around the statue, and the crystal quartz must be put on the feet of statue or fetish too. Meditate so deeply for about 20 minutes, having a complete and total control about your thoughts and visualizing a black and red light descending into the statue or fetish one. When you think you are ready, let's vibrate the following mantra in front of the statue as many times as you think is good for you. The idea is to be in primordial gnosis with the realms of death, letting the queen of darkness and guardian of cemetery cover you with its flame of knowledge and teach you the gardens of bones and the tree of darkness though its presence.

Mantra:
VENID -REMUTE- MUERTE -NEVID

After this, keep on repeating the mantra and get the crystal quartz and hold on in your left hand, so through this symbolism you are now the left hand of the reaper; you are the key to its most hidden mysteries of death and rebirth, you are now a vulture eating the carrion of dead shells, and you're now a portal to influx of such energies. Put the crystal on the altar again and let's get the magickal rosary and chant in a slow way the following invocation:

> *Hail Mother death, hail mother of darkness*
> *Bring me to your kingdom of deads,*
> *In the dark bark of emptiness, hail mother death*
> *Bring me to the seas of hidden knowledge*
> *Show me the path of your inner worlds oh Queen*
> *Of the night, death bringer.*
> *Drunk me with your presence oh Mother Death*
> *To me, to me, come to me oh mother death*
> *Reveal to me the pathways of hidden light*
> *Pierced in me, the claws of death with your poisonous lips!!*
> *Hail mother death, I chant for you in this darken night!!*

After a moment just visualize the image of La Santisima Muerte burning in a radiant dark purple light. Then start to visualize how such radiant light enters your body via anja chakra until you feel you have absorbed enough energy from La Santisima. Once the vision is finished, you can relax for some minutes, controlling your breaths, and repeat 2 times!

Ave mother of darkness and death, the work is complete!!

Pick up your ritual elements and leave the cemetery fields.

MEDITATION

You can imagine walking in the desert at night, and a tall shape of death dressed in black coming to you with a blood-red book in hand. As the shape is nears, you can feel the necessity to get connected with its essence and learn the mysteries of dead realms. You took the book and fully concentrated in each one of the pages, full of invocations and rituals.

With this meditative trip the sorcerer moves so deeply into the archetypal world of hidden consciousness, letting you to know more about the strong archetypical shape of death, going deep in the meanings of his black clothes, its deep black hole eyes, its pale skeletal body and dark nature.

RITUAL OF DESTRUCTION

The following ritual is used for curse or to destroy an enemy causing him/her diseases, mental illness or even suffering and death.

Implements:
- 1 Black Candle
- Sigil Of Destruction
- Incense Of Saturn
- La Santisima Muerte fetish or statue

Prepare carefully the ritual chamber or place in/outside for the ritual. For experience, I just prefer to work outside, near a river, a forest or, much better, in a cemetery at sunset. Let's start with the ritual adapting the altar with your fetish or statue of La Santisima Muerte, with the death rosary around its body. The Saturn Incense must be burnt and to create a proper atmosphere to the ritual itself, so I mean you should include some ritual music.

Burn the black candle from the fetish or statue, and whispering, you cry:

"Oh holy mother of the dead"

And while you are burning the candle, you focus and concentrate on the flame, visualizing a black flame rising around a purple fog emanating into the statue or fetish. Following this, you get the death rosary from the statue or fetish and start chanting or whispering

"Ave Madre Muerte, Ave Queen Of Darkness, Ave Holy Death"

Try to chant this in a strong intonation, while you visualize the black flame burning and looking how the scythe starts shining. After some minutes you put the death rosary around your neck and follow this invocation:

Oh Queen Of the Death, Mother Of Darkness
I invoke your most baneful and malefic aspects
In order to help me to destroy my enemies
Assist me with your lethal poison, to cause suffering &
pestilence to my enemies
Drain its energies oh queen of darkness, oh mother of death

While doing the invocation, draw a sigil of your own choice on a piece of paper and repeat 7 times:

Assist me mother of death, Queen of darkness it let be done
Salve mother of death, Salve queen of the dead

Let's burn the sigil in the black candle, and the ritual is finished!

THE TRIUMPH OF DEATH

Claudio Carvalho

This is a good opportunity for there to be some interesting clarification on the Triumph so controversial in the Book of Thoth, called Death.

Many things are said about the Death in regard to its mystical, superstitious, and alchemical contexts, among other considerations. Generally speaking about Death, there is something both intriguing and scary because you do not know what's on the 'other side' or 'beyond' of life.

Since old times, much has been studied and talked about this delicate subject; however, both conceptions such as vulgar and scatological on Death mingled in an uncontrolled manner and this junction there were several misconceptions and superstitions that astray concepts more internal than she really means, and we have left on your actual reading is included in the symbolism and iconography of various prints and paintings done in the Middle Ages through the freshness Renaissance that rescued the oldest myths of Greece and by converging detailed Baroque allegory where it was developed for new gloomy and hidden traces from the Hermetic Romantic Tradition.

Even in the midst of such transformations, Death always held she Dance, adapting to cultural customs that always march to dispose of her *Triumph*.

Although this theme is much older than the period that this essay will cover, remains testify that the richest time concerning Death is the Middle Ages and the Renaissance, which therefore represent both an equivocal understanding and a natural attraction that hugged the minds of these two periods.

Humanists from years *Trecento*, such as François Rabelais († 1553), Francesco Petrarca († 1374), and Giovanni Boccaccio († 1375) to name a few, all have relied much on the writings of Florentine poet Dante Alighieri († 1321), mainly in the wonderful work called *The Divine Comedy*, which describes the rise of a wanderer to the top of his initiation through three aspects of Death. These humanists had a strong influence on literature and painting at that time; for example, Petrarch, a great scholar, circa 1356 wrote a beautiful poem called *Il Trionphi*, depicting allegories through triumphal processions in their secular six letters: Trumps, Love (the Lovers), Chastity (Temperance), Death, Fame (the Chariot), Time (the Hermit) and Eternity (the World). There is even a theory about the etymology of the word Trump given to the Major Arcana, attributed the title of the poem by Petrarch, and others as Jacopo Antonio Marcello, a spokesman of the fifteenth century.

Some research of the history of the Tarot is based on the creation of the thirteenth card through a distinct drama from the liturgical cycle that is naturally called several names, *The Dance of Death*, *The Dance Macabre*, etc. This drama was probably encouraged by the Black Death that devastated Europe between 1347 and 1364 C.E. The occurrence of this fact was due to the enormous difficulty that existed as hygiene among Europeans, unlike the East whose cleanliness was highly appreciated, proliferated the epidemic throughout most of the West.

The Dance of Death draws man's attention to more spiritual matters, not frivolousness that embraced many due to dissatisfaction existing in those times leading many people to debauchery in order to counter a dogmatic and dictator concept and that means enforcing the religious population. The mortuary symbolism that connotes Death exists for all classes or independent hierarchies, and that nothing leads to another world except your moral and righteous actions, and this was the pictorial view represented in the *Cimetière des Saints-Innocents* in Paris, which qualifies all social classes, such as the Pope, the Emperor, the Beggar, the Fool, the Hermit and others so that nothing escapes Death.

VARIATIONS FROM THE DANCE OF DEATH

Many versions from the Dance of Death were painted by numerous writers in the Netherlands, Germany and Belgium. Her fascination persists to modern times, and tends to continue.

In his Divine Comedy, Dante in 'Purgatory' faces Death when he pleads guilty, and so Mathilde dips him into Lethes in order to purify him. This confession was necessary so that Dante could continue on his path that would lead him to Paradise by Beatrice, his Essence. At this time he was prepared for his first death and right now it is recited:

> "Mathilde, opening her arms suddenly
> She girded my forehead and sudden sank me;
> It was of this water that I to draw from conveniently"[1].

Analogous to Dante, another great poet, writer and English painter, William Blake († 1827) wrote "The Couch of Death" published on Poetry and Prose of William Blake. It is a story with strong gothic influence. Amid a dense forest with nocturnal animals lurking, a family gathered around the bed of a diseased, about to leave his weakened body when he speaks about his departure and Death as well:

> "I walk in regions of Death, Where no tree is;
> Without a lantern to direct my steps,
> Without a staff to support me"

Nevertheless, in the end, his Dance of Death was comforted by angels enabling a young person a pleasant departure for eternity. Another facet of her eternal dance is published in Flowers of Evil, written by the poet and writer Charles-Pierre Baudeleire († 1867), that devoted his passion towards a mulatto woman named Jeanne Duval in 1857. In his twenty-ninth poem entitled "The Dancing Serpent" he glimpses the seductive power of Death as a serpent *that sows the stars in your soul*. At one of the stanzas is written:

> "To see you walk in cadence,
> Fair unconstrained, brings to mind,
> A serpent dancing at the prodding of a stick."

As you can see, the content of the verses from the nineteenth century already has a format of "movement" for Death, not as a triumphal procession,

---

[1] There are some books whose quotes are on the original in Portuguese, so in these versions the author himself decided to translate them to English-speaking readers.

but as seduction of internal metamorphosis succumbing to any desire for the Sacred or longing for God, wishing for his intoxicating Beloved who shines in front of the Inner Temple, the primordial waters of the Self.

Somewhat occurs here a need to return to the hermetic principle that, unlike the Tarot cards of the past, now shows a more complex symbology and directed to Qabalistical and alchemical contexts so loveable to romantic Hermetists. Julius in his book The Hermetic Tradition develops the rescue alchemical well when he says:

> "Now the whole secret of the first phase of the hermetic Opus
> consists in this:
> In working in such a way that the consciousness is not
> reduced and then suspended
> At the threshold of sleep, but instead can accompany this
> process through all its
> Phases, in complete awareness, up to a condition
> equivalent to death. The "disso-
> lution" is then made into a living, intense, indelible
> experience, and this is the
> Alchemical "death," the "blacker than black," the entrance
> into the "tomb of Osiris,"
> The knowledge of the dark land, the realm of Saturn, of
> which the texts speak."

After Evola tells us above, the Portuguese bard called Fernando Pessoa does an amazing Ode in Obra Poética interpreting the single moment of Death as a solemn prostration before the Silence, so he reiterates:

> "When I die,
> When I'm gone, ignobly, like everyone else,
> For that way down whose idea you cannot face the front,
> Through that door to which, if we could loom up, could not
> loom up,
> For that harbor which the captain's ship does not know,
> Be for this time decent of boredom that I had,
> By this mystical and spiritual time and most ancient,

*By this time that perhaps there is much more time than
it seems
Plato dreaming saw the mind of God
Body sculpting and existence sharply plausible
Within his thought externalized as a field"[2].*

As the attentive reader may notice, the continued Dance of Death slips all the time in our lives, consciously or not, and she's always one step away from us, to kiss and embrace, in a mad frenzy of delight.

Another who felt the cold breath of sweet Death was Oscar Wilde[3]. A poet, playwright and writer, he edited a wonderful collection of poems called Rosa Mystica and her Requiescat Complete Works. In it he states:

*"She that was young and fair,
Fallen to dust,
Lily-like, white as snow,
She hardly knew
She was a woman, so
Sweetly she grew.
Peace, Peace, she cannot hear
Lyre or sonnet,
All my life's buried here
Heap earth upon it."*

Aleister Crowley († 1947), in his exceptional collection so-called Collected Works of Aleister Crowley, in 1907, writes in "Gargoyles - Images of Death" a litany for Kali which is one of the verses recited as follows:

*Death from the universal force,
Means to the forceless universe, Birth.
I accept the furious course,
Invoke the all-embracing curse,
Blessing and peace beyond may lie,
When I annihilate the "I." (Kali)*

---

[2] Translation by the author from Portuguese version.
[3] Oscar Fingal O'Flahertie Wills Wilde was born in Dublin on 16 October 1854 and died in Paris on November 30, 1900

Various religious traditions revere the myth and their ancestral gods, and this goes beyond when they invoke the Celtic tradition with their four hundred gods and goddesses or more that overflow in a mixture of tragedy and heroism, and one of its biggest heirs arises from the Arthurian legends, also known as Merlin or Myrddin; he offers a treat in his Dance of Death in the poem "Song of Taliesin" published in The 21 Lessons of Merlin and singing thus:

> *"I have been a fierce Bull and a yellow buck.*
> *I have been a boat upon the sea.*
> *I have been the foam of water.*
> *I have been a drop in the air.*
> *I have journeyed high as an eagle."*

The Dance of Death refutes fleeting relationships in favor of life to what is deepest in us, touching us and awakening us to a single direction and no deviations towards total awareness of who we really are. She makes us realize the vulgarization that embraces the way of life of the human being, and this theme, although secular, it is extremely present in many senses. This conception of time, behold iconographic variations arise in the Tarot cards as a whole, and in the case of Death these variations sound provocative and challenging to men in order to not underestimate her Triumphal power.

ICONOGRAPHY OF DEATH

The iconographic variation from Death Tarot cards suggests a certain way, cultural and religious aspects in force at a particular time of the making of images to be recorded in woodcut or etching determining the shapes and lines that played the tarotiers[4] in their respective record of centuries Tarot cards.

Just as there was the development of the point of view of Death, its iconography has generated interesting paintings from the time of Duccio di Buoninsegna, founder of the School of Siena and Giotto, as well as other authors like Petrarch, Boccaccio, Ghiberti and Leonardo Vasari, and preserved the anonymity until the paintings from Pamela Colman Smith and Lady Frieda Harris in the twentieth century.

---

[4] They are a kind of goldsmiths who elaborated the tarot cards.

The older Tarot cards accounted Death naked, only the skeleton with her sickle, sometimes on foot or horseback. Later, some packs placed in a hood or robe, in other armor as Waite's Tarot. He said in his The Pictorial Key to the Tarot there was need for a correction on this card:

"The veil or mask of life perpetuated in change, transformation
And passage from lower to higher, at this is more fitly
Represented in the rectified Tarot by one of the apocalyptic
Visions than by the crude notion of the reaping skeleton"

Liz Greene and Juliet Sharman-Burke in The Mythic Tarot use their cards based on the Greek model for hieratic images, if they chose to Death the god Hades, the Lord of the Underworld or subconscious. In her pictograph Death uses a helmet covering her face along with a black robe covering her entire body. Perhaps she is indicating the silence that exists behind each inner transformation.

According to Stuart Kaplan in Tarot Classic, there is an interesting symbolism for the skeleton in which he says:

"The energy of the skeleton acts as a destructive force
That serves to break the chains that prevent
And obstruct the changes. Fear of change often obscures
The promise of a new direction and opportunities
That await the person be able to change the direction of your
life" [5].

Papus in The Tarot of the Bohemians from another perspective complements what said Kaplan with his statement:

"The Works of the head (conception) become immortal
As soon as they are realized (heads and feet)."

There is an alchemical process that runs subtly Death Trump that is part of the continuous development of all things that exist in the universe, from the smallest particle of matter to the widest that may exist, a power that confuses many scholars, researchers and Hermetists, which is summarized in

---

[5] Translation by the author from Portuguese version.

Transmutatio, something far beyond that inherent in the transformation of its rich image. Some call Transmutatio Virium or Transmutation Forces as would say Mouni Sadhu in his work called The Tarot. The myriad forms are but transitory, since man has the power both to mask them as to transmute them and so can become an inexhaustible source of emotional and psychic being overwhelmed by his personality or distill it and transforming your personal valours, expanding your consciousness to attain a state of empty and become One in It-self, i.e. UNO.

Crowley in The Book of Thoth identified this Transmutatio with the glyph of the Eagle, which is more representative of sublimated aspect of Scorpio, the sign that typifies Death. He explains:

> *"The highest aspect of the card is the Eagle,*
> *This represents exaltation above solid matter."*

He continues:

> *"The card itself represents the dance of death;*
> *The figure is a skeleton bearing a scythe,*
> *And both the skeleton and scythe are*
> *Importantly Saturnian symbols."*

Saturn represents the Time (Tempus), but in another respect extols the interval between one cycle and another, a kind of contraction time, and it resides when the polarities are neutralized in an exact moment like eternity, and this indicates a characteristic worldview from Zen schools.

Oswald Wirth possibly realized something close it when he drafted the Thirteenth Trump of his deck. He relied on the cards of the Tarot du Marseille, mainly in the pictograph deck produced by Nicholas Conver; however, he joined the image of some letters to the tarotic teachings of Eliphas Levi Zahed († 1875). One of the greatest expressions of Levi in your deck is seen in both Trumps VII (the Chariot) and XV (the Devil), the latter typifying the hieratic figure of Baphomet shown in Dogma and Ritual of High Magic. However, the thirteenth Trump, Death has a smiling face indicating an ecstasy in decapitating the weaknesses of men in order to transform them properly into the next phase of their initiation, which will rectify it as drinking some of the Elixir of Life, but can exist life after death? Behold the confusion of many.

Wirth with his Death Trump, most likely relied on pictographic style in Tarocco Piemontese, prepared some years before the making of his deck as it is explained in I Tarocchi. Storia Arte Magia.

Many of the romantic time decks were idealized from subtle indications of previous decks though there is a clear difference between them. Many tarologists should know there is not necessarily a division of the path taken by both decks, from medieval to seventeenth-century after those fruitful romanticism of Antoine Court Gebelin († 1784), obviously that certain symbols were recovered and brought the surface while others were rectified; however, Death is more complete and ballet dancing triumphantly in her wonderfully harmonious rhythm was painted by Lady Frieda Harris in the Thoth Tarot. And it is with her that we complete this short essay on One that is most feared and most beloved of all human fears, The Divine Death.

> *"Death brings me a slight feeling of freshness,*
> *Mow me her passion and longing,*
> *For our souls is One on One,*
> *And our hearts are destroyed,*
> *By dread that elevates me to a new landscape,*
> *The strength of her Love for me,*
> *Passed on into single kiss,*
> *Myself forever"* [6].

BIBLIOGRAPHY

Alighieri, Dante: Divina Comedia. Traducção Brasileira de José Pedro Xavier Pinheiro: 2ª edição. Cuidadosamente revista, accrescida com setenta e cinco estampas de GUSTAVO DURÉ, enriquecida com um autographo do Traductor e acompanhada de um completo RIMARIO organisado pelo filho do Traductor Xavier Pinheiro (J.A.), I Volume. Editor Jacintho Ribeiro dos Santos. 1918: Rio de Janeiro.

---

[6] From my authorship.

Baudelaire, Charles-Pierre: As Flores do Mal. Círculo do Livro S.A.: 1981. São Paulo.

Blake, Willian: Poetry and Prose of Willian Blake. The Centenary Edition of Blake's Poetry and Prose. Edited by Geoffrey Keynes. Complete in one volume. The Nonesuch Library. 1956: London.

Burke-Sharman, Juliet e Liz Greene: O Tarô Mitológico, uma nova abordagem para a leitura do Tarô. Edições Siciliano: 1990. São Paulo.

Chevalier, Jean e Alain Gheerbrant: Diccionario de los Símbolos. Editorial Herder S.A.: sd. Barcelona.

Crowley, Aleister: Collected Works of Aleister Crowley. With portraits. Volume III. Foyers Society for the Propagation of Religious Truth. [1907]. rpt. by Yogi Publication Society: sd. Illinois.

The Book of Thoth (Egyptian Tarot) by Master Therion. Samuel Weiser, Inc.: 1969, rpt. 1996: Maine. Também traduzido em português como (O Livro de Thoth), Editora Madras Ltda e Anúbis Editores Ltda: 2000. São Paulo. The Crowley Tarot, the handbook to the cards by Aleister Crowley and Frieda Harris. Arranged and Foreword by Akron and Hajo Banzhaf. U.S.Games Systems, Inc.: 1995. Stamford. CT.

Thoth Tarot Deck: Designed by Aleister Crowley and artist executant, Frieda Harris. Distributed by Samuel Weiser, 734 Broadway, N.Y. 10003, Printed in U.S.A. [1969].

Thoth Tarot Deck: Designed by Aleister Crowley and painted by Lady Frieda Harris. Booklet of Instructions [Two essays by Lady Frieda Harris & foreword by S.R. Kaplan]. Complete 78-Card Crowley Tarot Deck in stunning new edition based upon the original pintings. Cards printed in Belgium. Booklet and box printed in U.S.A. Published and distributed by U.S. Games, Inc: 1978. New York

Thoth Tarot Deck: In small card size. Booklet of Instructions [Includes essays by Lady Frieda Harris and foreword by Stuart R. Kaplan]. Complete 80-Card Crowley Tarot Deck Includes Three Renditions of The Magus/Magician Cards. Published and distributed by U.S. Games Systems, Inc, Stamford and AGMüller & CIE, Switzerland: 1986.

Ediciones del Prado: História Geral da Arte. Arquitetura, Escultura, Pintura e Artes Decorativas. Dicionário Biográfico de Artistas I (A-K). Fernado Chinaglia Distribuidora S.A.: 1996. Rio de Janeiro.

Evola, Julius: A Tradição Hermética. Nos seus Símbolos, na sua Doutrina, e na sua Arte Régia. Edições 70: 1979. Lisboa.

Huson, Paul: Mystical Origins of the Tarot. From Ancient Roots to Modern Usage. With ilustrations by the author. Destiny Books: 2004. Vermont.

Kaplan, Stuart R.: Tarô Clássico. Cartas vindas do passado revelam o futuro. Um guia definitivo e profissionalmente ilustrado do Tarô. Editora Pensamento Ltda: 1983. São Paulo.

Levi, Eliphas: Dogma e Ritual da Alta magia. Editora Pensamento S.A.: 1974. São Paulo

Monroe, Douglas: The 21 Lessons of Merlin. A Study in Druid Magic & Lore. Llewellyn Publications: 1996. Minnesota.

Papus: El Tarot De Los Bohemios. Clave absoluta de la Ciencia oculta. Editorial Kier, S.A.: 1970. Buenos Aires.

Pessoa, Fernando: Obra Poética. Em um volume. Editora Nova Aguilar S.A.: 1986. Rio de Janeiro.

Sadhu, Mouni: O Tarô, manual prático de ocultismo. Editora Siciliano: 1993. São Paulo.

Vitali, Andrea e Zanetti, Terri: I Tarocchi. Storia Arte Magia dal XV al XX secolo. Edizioni LE TAROT: 2006. Ravenna.

Waite, Arthur E.: The Pictorial Key to the Tarot. Being Fragments of a Secret Tradition Under the Veil of Divination. With 78 plates, illustrating the Greater and Lesser Arcana, from Designs by Pamela Colman Smith. Introduction by Paul M. Allen. Rudolf Steiner Publications: 1971. New York.

Tarô. A Sorte Pelas Cartas. Constando de fragmentos de Uma Tradição Secreta Sob o Véu da Advinhação. Com 78 gravuras ilustrando os Grandes e Pequenos Arcanos. Editora Tecnoprint S.A.: 1985. São Paulo.

Produced by Frankie Albano. (Albano-Waite). This Tarot was created by Arthur Edward Waite and artistically painted by Pamela Colman Smith. Published by TAROT PRODUCTIONS, Inc: 1968. Los Angeles.

Wirth, Oswald: The Original and only authorized Oswald Wirth Tarot Deck. Made in Switzerland by AGMüller. Distributed exclusively by U.S. Games, Inc: 1976. Stamford.

Wilde, Oscar: Obra Completa. Em um volume. Editôra José Aguilar, Ltda: 1961. Rio de Janeiro.

DISCOGRAPHY

Theatre of Tragedy: Velvet Darkness They Fear. Massacre Records: 1996. California.

Arutam, Muisak, Nekas: "Three Souls Of The Shuar"

Andrew Dixon & Sarah Price

T he Shuar people of the Amazon, more commonly known as the Jivaro, are best known in Western cultures for their creation of shrunken heads properly called tsantsa by the Shuar tribespeople. These extraordinary physical representations of the culture of the Shuar are based on and a result of their belief in three distinctly separate types of souls, or wakanï. These are the arutam wakanï, also known as the ancient spectre soul, believed to protect the possessor from physical harm; this is an acquired soul, and a person may have up to two of these souls at any one time. The muisak wakanï is also an acquired soul but one which is created by the murder—by physical or magical means—of a person, and its existence is simply to gain revenge for the death. For this reason, the muisak wakanï is known as the avenging soul. The nékas wakanï is the ordinary soul, which is born with the person but which continues to exist after that person's death.

The existence of these three kinds of souls and their acquisition in the case of the arutam and muisak mean that in Jivaro society the most proficient killers (known as kakaram) are highly revered, and with the shamans regularly used hallucinogenic drugs, such as datura and natemä, to access the supernatural world. So inherent is their belief in the invisible world being the true "reality" that within days of being born, a Jivaro baby will be given a hallucinogen to help it see and enter the "real" world in the hope that the child will see an "ancient spectre" to help it survive infancy. Even their hunting dogs are given a special hallucinogen to connect them to the supernatural plane.

It is the description of these three souls which the first part of this essay addresses. The second part describes a ritual undertaken many years ago, inspired by the study of the Jivaro tsantsa during my own forays into the Tunnels of Set following Kenneth Grant's *Nightside of Eden*.

ARUTAM SOUL

The "ancient spectre" soul, or arutam wakanï, is as described above believed by the Jivaro to be an acquired soul, and some begin to look to obtain them from childhood, as males of the tribe are not expected to live beyond puberty without having at least one. This is mainly due to the fact that murders between tribes is/was the main cause of violent death, and are usually directed toward men rather than women or children.

Waterfalls are particularly sacred to the Jivaro (they are also known as the "people of the sacred waterfalls"), as it is in the breezes around these that the spirits are most often found. Those seeking an arutam vision will spend time, up to five days, bathing in the waterfall, fasting and drinking water steeped in green tobacco. This is a procedure which if not successful will be repeated at a later date, or if the need to acquire an arutam wakanï is considered important enough, a more intense method may be used. The seeker may resort to drinking hallucinogenic juice, maikua, the most powerful drug known to the Shuar and known in Western cultures as datura.

After a few hours of drinking the juice of the plant, if lucky, the person will enter the hidden world of the spirits and "wake" in the night amidst a great storm, with thunder, lightning and winds powerful enough to fell trees, although the stars will be absent in this night's sky. The arutam if it appears can be in a variety of forms. It can look like a ball of fire, a human head or even in the shape of two spirit animals; pairs of jaguars or anacondas fighting are the most prevalent. These apparitions can be so fearsome that the tribesperson may sometimes run from it, but to gain an arutam soul they must go towards it and touch it either with their bare hand or a small stick (much like the "coup stick" of the North American Plains Indian). When this is achieved, the arutam vision will explode and vanish, leaving the seeker to return home. The next night they will dream of an old man who, from Michael J. Harner's *The Jivaro*, will speak to him: "I am your ancestor. Just as I have lived a long time so will you. Just as I have killed many times so will you." After which, he will vanish and the arutam wakanï will now reside in the dreamer's chest.

Having one arutam soul is said to protect the possessor from harm from magical attack, death from physical assault or from poisoning; a person who has two is also protected from disease and will not die from any reason while they are in his (or her) possession. While only having two such souls at one time is possible they are not, however, kept with the person for their lifetime, as after four or five years it is believed that the soul will leave and "wander off" into the jungle. They can also be stolen, usually by shamans, either for their own use or on the request of a warrior who is planning to kill the person owning the soul; of course, while still in possession of the arutam wakanï, the person cannot be killed. It is for this reason that a member of the Jivaro would not stop after having acquired only two souls, as after four years, or sooner if one or both souls were to be stolen, they would need to be replaced.

It is not only for protection either that the accumulation of arutam souls is desirable; when obtained they are said to increase the person's power (ka-karma) in many ways. The owner of the soul will feel stronger and more intelligent, make it harder for them to lie or perform acts which are considered dishonourable in the eyes of the Jivaro. While they are not to tell anyone of their arutam souls, or they will leave them, it is through their actions and abilities, their confidence and demeanour that others can know that they now hold one, or if it is subsequently lost.

Therefore over their lifetime, a Jivaro could possess many souls, and while only two may be held at any one time, when the next is taken it will aid the person in keeping the power of the previous soul, so that they gradually accumulate strength and energy through these practices.

One other attribute of acquiring an arutam wakanï, however, is that in most instances the successful seeker will be filled with a great desire to kill, and within months will join an expedition to another tribe with the sole purpose of committing murder. It is when this occurs that another form of soul comes into existence, the muisak.

Muisak Soul

The muisak is known as the avenging soul and comes into being upon the death by murder—including sorcery—of one who has possessed an arutam soul in their lifetime. In fact the number of arutam souls that they accumulated in their life will be created upon their death, natural or otherwise, to live on in the jungles and waterfalls before joining for a while with other Jivaro in the future.

At the point of death by murder, however, the muisak soul is formed and leaves the victim via the mouth and will try to exact revenge on the killer, or if they are protected by an arutam wakanï, upon their wife or family. To do this, the spirit will transform itself into one of three forms of demon or iwančï: either an anaconda or boa constrictor which would tip a raft on the river thus causing death, a poisonous snake to kill with its venom, or a tree to fall and crush the potential victim. It is believed the demon will only take one life, after which it will vanish and not kill again.

It is to counter this and protect themselves and their families that the Jivaro will take the head of their assassinated foe and use it to create the tsantsa, which capture and imprison the muisak, preventing it from performing its mission of revenge. The head is removed from the body and the skin cut up the back to make the removal of the skull easier; this cut is re-sewn and the skin is cleaned through boiling and repeatedly filling with hot stones and sand. Tar and charcoal is rubbed into the skin, and the eyes and mouth are sewn shut to thereby contain the avenging spirit until it can be dealt with when the Jivaro killing party returns home to its tribe.

Immediately after their return, there commences a period of feasting and dancing during which the power of the muisak can be transferred by the taker to others, usually women close to the killer. This is unlike the arutam soul, whose power can only be used by the one in which it is contained. During these feasts and celebrations of which there can be one but more typically three, the tribespeople are careful not to become involved in any fights or disagreements, as it is thought that the muisak will take the opportunity to escape from the binding which imprisons it within the tsantsa and commit murder.

At the end of the feasts, a banishing will take place and the muisak will be sent back to its place of origin. The shrunken head is now considered empty and of no spiritual value to the tribe, so can be freely passed on or sold. In rare cases the muisak will be kept bound within the tsantsa, usually by a shaman to be used in acts of sorcery.

NEKAS SOUL

The nékas wakanï is known as the true soul and unlike the arutam and muisak, is born with a person rather than being acquired and is viewed by the

Jivaro, as in many other cultures, as being linked with the blood. It is considered passive during a person's life and is not held in the same esteem as the other souls, and so it is not held in any deep regard or interest by the tribes. When it leaves the body after death, however, the nékas wakanï then goes through a variety of transformations.

In its first iteration, the soul leaves the host body in an invisible but identical form and moves to a spirit house, which is exactly the same as the person's when they were born. All deceased members of the tribe will be there, and the spirit will go through the person's normal activities as in life and will move as he/she did, effectively reliving the entire life span again as a ghost or "human demon". These souls, by going through the motions of eating, drinking, etc. are always unfulfilled and hungry, and are sometimes seen as pairs of owls and deer in abandoned sites. Once the entire lifetime has been repeated, the true soul will change again from a "human demon" into a "true demon", in which form it is visible, though reputedly ugly and alone, wandering the forest desperate for the company of others. Again, the life span is "lived" out and another form is taken—a large butterfly or moth. These are not feared? By the Jivaro as they may be the soul of an ancestor and as they are again considered to be always hungry, an offering of sweet manioc tubers or manioc beer will be made to them.

After a time, this form will fall to the ground and die, when its wings are damaged by the rain and the true soul will turn to water vapour. It will go through no more changes and will exist forever as mist, fog and clouds.

THE RITUAL

After having studied the Jivaro/Shuar for some time and been allowed access to several authentic tsantsa by the Pitt Rivers Museum in Oxford, I was inspired to create a similar entity. This came during a period when I was experimenting and exploring in the Tunnels of Set using Kenneth Grant's *Nightside of Eden*; I was focusing on the 24th Tunnel sentinelled by Niantiel, and the death symbolism and the influence of Scorpio inherent in this region seemed entirely suitable for such an endeavour, with its links to necromantic sorcery and zombieism.

From Kenneth Grant's *Nightside of Eden* (p222-223) describing an Atlantean ritual of zombification: "The zombie produced in this was not a soulless mechanism—as in the case of a zombie produced by Haitian Voodoo—but a highly intelligent *though automatic* entity combining the vividness and plasticity of astral consciousness with the magical qualities of the Adept himself. It was literally a child of the dead yet equipped with magical powers and with all the faculties of humanity except that of the Will."

And from Linda Falorio's *The Shadow Tarot*: "Here is the Black Temple Work of Atlantean Magicks, devolved into death cults which survive into the present time. Here are cults of magical cannibalism, of shrunken heads, of necrophilia with souls newly released by death for creation of astral zombies."

For this entity I obtained a replica tsantsa from Ecuador which would provide the physical shell to contain the spirit.

While waiting for the tsantsa to arrive, a ritual space was prepared and a sigil of Niantiel was "painted in lurid indigo brown—'like a black beetle'—on an indigo triangle on greenish blue"[1] and charged with blood. Graveyard dirt was spread around in the temple space, as were bones and various images of Death. On the altar the bodies of a beetle and a scorpion were laid just below where the tsantsa would be placed. Below these, plates and bowls were left with offerings of food, fruit and flowers left to rot and putrefy; these would be my incense for this rite. Five candles were used: three black, one white, one yellow. From Aleister Crowley and Lady Frieda Harris's the ATU XIII Death was used on and as a guardian for the doorway. Also in preparation, visits were paid to places of death, graveyards, sites of plague pits and

---

[1] Kenneth Grant, Nightside of Eden, p219

scenes of murder where offerings were made and in some instances tokens (flowers, a stone) were taken and left at the altar.

The tsantsa arrived and was place on the altar with the charged sigil of Niantiel. Five consecutive nights were assigned for the ritual's completion.

The first evening after bathing I entered the ritual space and lit the candles, and the names of the qlipha Niantiel were repeated as a mantra over and over while I began using Karezza, masturbating to the point of ejaculation but without release. This was continued long into the night while I focused on the sigil and attempted to move into and beyond it. Eventually tiredness and exhaustion left me unable to continue, and I closed the rite in preparation for the next day.

The second night followed the way of the first with the rite being concluded with no discernible result.

Continuing on the third night, I again began my mantra and within moments of starting Karezza, went into a meditative/trance state with an almost physical jolt and while looking at the Niantiel sigil, had the sensation of being simultaneously pulled towards it while being pushed away. When trying to describe the feeling later, I could only say that my eyeballs felt as though they had shot forward, reversed themselves, gone back and reversed themselves again as they returned to my sockets. This feeling of movement while not moving will of course be familiar to those who practise any form of meditation or ritual. While in the Tunnels of Set, I found that opposing experiences would occur with great regularity and quite often be an indicator of having entered one of the Tunnels; loud thunderous noise and total silence existing in my consciousness together was a frequent occurrence.

Directly after this, the painted sigil—the focus of my attention—seemed both clearer and further away; as the evening continued my trance state deepened and expanded. The room, while small, seemed extensive, its boundaries no longer limited. A nimbus of rainbow-like colours seemed to form a halo around the image, although I could not honestly say if my eyes were still open at this point. There was a feel of movement around me, of furred things rustling but making no noise. The floor/ground was covered with small snakes also hazy, shimmering, iridescent and rainbow-coloured.

I attempted to move my focus to the tsantsa; without speaking or moving, I tried to indicate my intent for an entity to inhabit this shell. Unlike the rituals performed by the Jivaro to keep and contain a muisak wakanï (avenging soul) of a murder victim, I was hoping to induce a willing entity into this form. This only continued, however, for a short period. Fading, drawing away and darkening while becoming more solid and substantial, the room around me was somehow less. Almost too tired to move and shaking with exhaustion, but exceedingly pleased, I closed down the ritual for the night and slept.

Fourth night. Enthused by the previous evening, I began again and this time the entry into the 24th Tunnel was easier—something akin to going down a slide—although the discomfort of moving/not moving was still there and imparted a feeling of nausea. By degrees both the room and my consciousness seemed to expand; there was the feeling of being watched and the impression of movement again, still silent. Vague geometric shapes or firework explosions seemed distant and faint, then the impression of fading into a jungle, and now there was noise, chatter, clucking, shrieking—not overpowering but continuous. Creatures/entities seemed to be just beyond eyesight or view, and I had no impression of the room I was in at all, as I now stood and turned around, glimpsing movement but not seeing. In the way I had done previously I sent out my invitation, visualising rather than verbalising. I kept turning and saw part of the foliage was pushed aside, and a fur-covered figure came before me on all fours: a sloth.[2] In my head I only heard a name "Mattie".

Final, fifth night. After closing the ritual the previous night, I had known I had found the entity which would inhabit the tsantsa. "He" had accepted the invitation to inhabit the shrunken head, to be provided for and to provide services. This had been achieved without conversation but with complete understanding. I had closed the ritual and sat in the room resting—even then the shell which would come to contain Mattie, at least in part, seemed to be now something more than just an object.

With blood and oils, the tsantsa was sigilised and blessed; this time again with comparative ease I slipped into the Tunnel sentinelled by Niantiel to complete the last part of the ritual. This time I held with my right hand the shrunken head. The "feel" of the Tunnel was similar, and although I had the impression of being in a jungle or forest, it was one of blackness with everything still clear and visible (there was no sun, sky or moon). Mattie and I met, and though as described different, we were in the same place; our agreement was confirmed, and I traced the sigil I had used on the tsantsa on

---

[2] Sloths and monkeys are both used by the Jivaro to practise their head-shrinking techniques.

his forehead. Leaving the Tunnel, while not hard, was a different experience this time—jagged and uneven rather than something smoothly fading as experienced before, but the rite was closed and Mattie and I left the ritual space together.

Andrew Dixon & Sarah Price

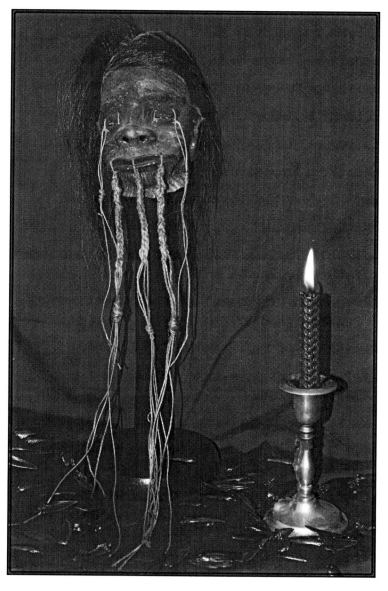

BIBLIOGRAPHY

Bertiaux, Michael: Voudon Gnostic Workbook, Magickal Childe Inc., 1988

Brujo Negro: Voodoo Sorcery Grimoire, Scientists of New Atlantis, Palm Springs, 2000

Castaneda, Carlos: The Teachings of Don Juan, Penguin Books, 1970

Tales of Power, Penguin Books, 1976

A Separate Reality, Penguin Books, 1977

Journey to Ixtlan, The Lessons of Don Juan, Penguin Books, 1994

Falorio, Linda: The Shadow Tarot, Aeon Books Ltd, 2004

Grant, Kenneth: Cults of the Shadow, Frederick Muller, London, 1975

Nightside of Eden, Frederick Muller, London, 1977

Outside the Circles of Time, Frederick Muller, London, 1980

Hall, Nicholas: Chaos and Sorcery, Published by Nicholas Hall, 1992

Harner, Michael J: The Jivaro, People of the Sacred Waterfalls, Robert Hale and Company, London, 1973

Sennitt, Stephen: Dark Doctrines, The Nox Anthology, New World Publishing, Yorkshire, 1991

Monstrous Cults, New World Publishing, Yorkshire, 1992

Svoboda, Robert E: Aghora, Brotherhood of Life Publishing, Albuquerque, 1986

Aghora II: Kundalini, Brotherhood of Life Publishing, Albuquerque, 1993

Aghora III: The Law of Karma, Brotherhood of Life Publishing, Albuquerque, 1997

Up de Graff, F W: Head Hunters of the Amazon. Seven Years of Exploration and Adventure, Garden City Publishing, New York, 1923

Wendell, Leilah: The Necromantic Ritual Book, Westgate Press, New Orleans, 1991

Our Name is Melancholy, Westgate Press, New Orleans, 1992

"In The Garden Of Bones: Working With Death & The Dead In Pan-Aeonic Witchcraft"

Bradley Allen Bennett

I
Introduction

"For rebellion [is as] the sin of witchcraft, and stubbornness [is as] iniquity and idolatry..."

—1 Sa 15:23 KJV

I ntroductions are in order, both for my avowedly stubborn and rebellious person and this thing I'm calling "PAN-Aeonic Witchcraft". Only a few of you will ever have heard of me before now. I come from relatively unknown quarters. I am Bradley Allen Bennett, known also as Two Crows, Frater Uraeus 161, and previously as NVD 111. The other numerous nicknames, nom de plumes, and handles I've wielded and answered to over the years are immaterial to this work, but stories in themselves. To most directly addresses, via an intentionally mixed metaphor, the four-hundred-pound pink elephant in the room—I do in fact think of myself as another incarnation of my namesake. Having mastered the Wand, I have returned now to master the Chalice and share the mysteries of the Jar of our Mother PANDORA via the Uncoiling of VIGEROS into the present space-time.

Because of my uniquely personal spiritual and magikal journey, I'm not always quite sure how to present myself when the obligatory religion-tradition questions arise. Most labels fail miserably to convey the essence of my experiences. It really cannot be otherwise for anyone and pat answers halt discussions with assumptive nods. Those labels I claim for myself I do so on my own terms. I eschew terminological straight-jackets and notions of proprietary definitions in the face of evident broader usages. I have found that groups of "like mind" all too often rim the pitfall of groupthink. Labels seem too often to bypass the patient processes that lead to understanding and onwards to wisdom. Dangerously entrenched literalism often comes from conceptual fixations and the inability to break free from the fetters of symbolic language. Joseph Campbell poignantly framed it as the mistake of conflating poetry with prose. On one of another hands, it is also via language constructs that magickal engines can be fashioned which are able to propel us into places beyond the words of tongues and waking minds.

At the same tender age that I discovered that there was such a thing as religion in the world, it was painfully evident that not everyone accepted each other under whatever labels their adherences left them stuck with or that they chose via the herding instinct. In the dominant society of my youth, being rejected by any number of religious adherents meant only one thing—eternal damnation. It didn't matter which denomination I examined, they all had a hell for people not like them. Make no mistake; Occulture holds its own damnations and group norming in order to avoid them. I spent a season in the Baptist Temple doing my best to avoid Hell, and have paid those dues in full and then some. I have, afterwards, chosen to gladly accept whatever damnations are heaped upon me. I have joyously found Mother Hell among my greatest teachers.

PAN-Aeonic Witchcraft finds its way into the present Aeon via the monomythic journeys of individuals upon the Serpent Path, their delvings into unknown directions, and their willingness to assume the damnations of all authorities in heeding their own hidden gods. It represents the continuation of the fruits of at first seemingly ludicrous endeavors via the seeds of discontent, rebellion, and transgression, against the broad social fabric and also the occult institutions that have sometimes too easily and eagerly dismissed them. That line of heirloom seeds was first sown in preceding Aeons and carried forward by radical thinkers and doers. Their fresh fires from the heavens have brought us NU Aeons and worlds to explore. Their lineages are tangled and hidden, but the fruit is that selfsame forbidden in the garden. The threshold of the path leading thereunto is attended by dark and horrifying watchers, the narrow gate framed by Lust and Terror.

ΙΣΤΟΡΙΑ   HISTORIA

The relentless hunter of all that moves, constant shadow casting gloom; collector of all that breathes, and as sure as mother's womb, awaiting all the gateway to otherworld yawns wide the patient tomb. Priesthoods and statehoods mortal fears do perpetually groom, a garden of souls for power's sake ever greedily do they consume; In the blackest pit of hell alone through torments, flowers of eternal freedom brightly come to bloom.

Throughout the Aeons nothing has contributed more to the enterprising endeavors of magico-religion than the black-veiled mysteries of Death and what resides beyond the misty pale in that place untouched by glad sunlight. Nothing has stirred more terror in the beating human heart, instigated more hopeless clawing after immortality, or been any surer than the cold boney grip of Death dragging souls kicking and screaming into the great black unknown. Nothing has more murderously instigated the rending of souls from human flesh to render fuel for the fires of any number of Hells. All this and yet exploring the mysterious unseen worlds has been the business of Cunning Folk the world over, under any number of names. PAN-Aeonic Witch-Magi find themselves in the same ageless and dangerous pursuits. They cannot do otherwise.

The term "PAN-Aeonic" is not mine. As far as I can tell in my present state of education that term, at least as pertinent to this work, was coined by Nema of *Ma'at Magick* fame. The work of the Horus-Ma'at Lodge, with its numerous well-published Magi, is the primary source for the PAN-Aeonic conception as I am presently working it, but it is not the only one. An Aeon, in the sense presented here, comes via the Thelemic catena through Frater Achad and various Thelemic commentators from the Master Therion, and has roots in allusions to the Ritual Officers of the Hermetic Order of the Golden Dawn. Attendant to and informing that catena is a broader collection of conceptions owing roots to Jewish, Christian, Qabalistic, Gnostic, and Neo-Platonic sources. These reach even further into the history and archaeological record of Astrology and Calendrics in all its various applications. It stretches its tentacles into dozens of related subjects and sciences. Simply put, PAN-Aeonism is a rich, deep, and broad subject, for which I have only scratched the shallowest surface. If I have conceived of anything new, it is upon the shoulders of giants, and I yet return often to their fountains for inspiration.

Beginning sometime in the early nineties I became obsessed with eschatological mythologies and conceptions in every form I could uncover. I delved every source I could find, and I'm still not finished. What I was after at first was some sense of the inspirations of Apocalyptic and Pseudepigraphic Traditions in the canonical and apocryphal Judeo-Christian literary corpus, and their influences on modern Millennialism. My obsessive interests also included Astrological Ages and astronomical-calendrical calculations of the Age of Aquarius and the Kali Yuga. What I found was that this subject matter linked inseparably with a great many notions, some of which are seemingly central to a handful of distinctive cosmologies held in a variety of magico-religious traditions and associated sects. My research would eventually lead me to the work of Nema and the Horus-Ma'at Lodge, which seemed to hold the most advanced and balanced Thelemic Aeonic template. I still hold this view of the Ma'atian Aeonic Map, and it is one of the elements deeply informing my personal work. Another is the Cult of VIGEROS, with its Chthonic, Auranian, and Ophidian energetics.

If nothing else, I am a death-touched individual. At the age of six I experienced my first near-death experience in the throes of an encephalitic fever. I have held a Scorpionic fascination with Death and the Dead, the macabre, and the inner workings of living things from a young age. I have more than once played in graveyards, even as an adult. As an Emergency Medical Technician and Firefighter I handled the dead bodies of almost every conceivable form of demise, from the victims of murder, suicide, and automobile accidents, to those of burning, electrocution, dismemberment, drowning, and natural causes. I have more than once attended to dying human beings or even held them in my arms, from lovely old grandmothers having their last heart attacks to teenage suicides distraught over lost girlfriends. I have looked in the eyes of a burning man while wholly unable to rescue him and shortly afterwards called to give an account of his demise to his sorrow-stricken mother. I worked a city morgue contract for a few years in which I first encountered decomposed corpses and experienced the workings of a large city morgue, which was strangely like something out of a cliché television police serial. Beyond the physical and mundane aspects of my experiences with Death and the Dead, the unseen world has also pressed itself upon me. It is this aspect of my experiences that may prove the more interesting.

Among a host of other Spirits, the departed have penetrated my awareness in waking space-time and the between realms of dream, vision, and unlearned knowledge from a young age. I have routinely experienced presages of the deaths of all the members of my paternal side of the family and intermittently those of other relatives, friends, and a tiny handful of people unrelated to me. In popular paranormal parlance, "I see dead people" and not all of them know that they are dead. Some are certainly nicer than others. For a long time I was labored under the common conceptions of Spirits of all sorts, the Dead included. In time I learned to take them all the same way I take people, animals, and other aspects of reality, on their own terms without allowing the gossip and preconceptions to overly taint my own conclusions. We all have friends that others simply don't care for or outright hate. My Spirits are nothing different in that regard.

Roughly seven years ago now the stars conspired to bring together a small group of occultists that took the name of Ordo AShA. The fateful moment of impetus in the formation of this order took place behind the scenes of the Chthonic-Auranian Templars of Thelema at the suggestion of one of the Sovereigns, though he might not remember precisely the discussion in question or even the people involved. OAShA would go on to become the recipient of an ongoing series of messages from an alien intelligence known as VIGEROS. Whether at the hands of interpersonal will in the constellations of wandering stars or the nature of the messages themselves, all but two of the members of OAShA would eventually depart the order and go their separate ways shortly following a timed ritual to bring VIGEROS to Earth. One has taken the mantel of authority in the outer government of the order and is forever grateful for the love, soul honest wisdom, and selfless assistance of his friend in bringing VIGEROS forward into the light of awareness beyond the membership.

ΜΥΘΩΣ   MYTHOS

"Her gates are gates of death, and from the entrance of the house she sets out towards the underworld. None of those who enter there will ever return, and all who possess her will descend to the Pit." —The Seductress, Fragment 4Q184, Dead Sea Scrolls

This is the Year of the Witch, marked not just by the trisdecadic numerary nexus of the Common Era year, but the undeniable stirrings in the visions and works of those of the blood everywhere around the world. The Apocalypse has indeed dawned, raising the veil for those with eyes to see, ears to hear, and hearts worthy of carrying the mysteries of Witchcraft and low magick in their own Deepings in the manifest world. These strange souls are those that have accepted their gifts and curses, taken the Witches' Mark and enjoined the transgressive and Dionysian Serpent Path. They bear the stigmata that in the dominant society are the sure marks of damnation. In the sometimes relatively safer and lighter magical notions of Contemporary Paganism and Popular Wicca, they are often thought of as too dark, too dangerous, and perhaps wholly unacceptable. This up-swell in the energetics of Witchcraft is part of the evolution of the species and the unfolding of the Horian Word and Aeonic Zeitgeist. This Season of the Witch shall also mark the return of the Bird Serpent goddess from the dark depths of the all but forgotten Aeon of ISIS, bringing even further balance to the solar-phallic force and fire of the Hawk-headed god opening up NU vistas of exploration in the unseen worlds of the Lunar-Yonic and actively balanced alchemical-transformative syzygies of a variety of pairings beyond mere common gender duality.

The equinoctial changing of the gods has brought the Aeon of HORUS in which the basic unit of sovereignty is the individual and the words of the zeitgeist Thelema-Will-Agape-Love. Prior to that was the Aeon of OSIRIS which offered the words of obedience-duty-sin-damnation and the nation-states with their attendant state religions as the basic unit of sovereignty headed by god-kings and male demos-councils. The Aeon of MA'AT has also shown itself in the Double-Consciousness and Double Current of HORUS-MA'AT, with its truth, balance, and natural order, and in which the interplay between individual and the fabric of the cosmos, future, past, and present consciousnesses, in which sovereignty is forged in twining. Prior to the age of the Father and dying god-men was the Aeon of ISIS the Great Mother about which little is well known, and yet there are even still more Aeons. The Aeon following MA'AT has been contended as that of HRUMACHIS, while ambiguities surrounding the template of ritual officers and meaning of Liber AL are entertained by wise authorities and centers of pestilence alike. At the beginning of time, or perhaps the mythical age of eternal return, is offered the Aeon of the Dwarf BES in which the sovereignty would presumably be that of the individual or family, the latter favored by my own Spirits. Other Aeons and descriptions of those currently entertained include Nameless, Silent, Wordless, SET, the chaotic Pandaemonaeon, and one or two perhaps from my own inspirations, PAN and Enchirid-Aeon. Before these Aeons were many others in the maps of the Gnostics Valentinus and Basilides, and it is from those that we learn of SOPHIA, HOROS, and the Logos-Word that found its way into the Johannine works, possibly better attributed to Mary Magdalene. The word "Aeon" itself holds connections with the words Olam, Kalpa, Life, "Eternal Life", and the archaic Greek Aiwon, strangely similar to the name AIWASS. AION is also the Hellenistic god of Unbounded Time standing in the center of the Annulus of the Cosmos and the Zodiac. The imagery of the thirteenth standing at the center of the twelve, the center everywhere and the sphere the limits of which are nowhere found, are no feeble or useless allusions. They might perhaps offer a different perspective on the "scarcely a dozen magi" in the history of the world according to the confessions of Aleister Crowley.

ΘΕΩΡΙΑ   THEORIA

> "It is ... through the world of the imagination which takes us beyond the restrictions of provable fact, that we touch the hem of truth." —Madeleine L'Engle, A Circle of Quiet

There is an ancient and natural order evident in the multiverse. All sciences, even those of Scientific Illuminism and the artes thought primitive or superstitious by the dominant society, rest on the foundations of basic empirical methodologies. The key is methodologies, not a single method.

All maps, taxonomies, and axiomatic laws fail in the shifting of scale and context. Magick is no different. Mixing the planes is actually one method of magick. It is confusion of the planes, like the spacemarks, that is the pitfall.

PAN-Aeonic Witchcraft offers a suite of methodologies, an elastic and scalable modality all its own. It is not wholly unlike shifting methodologies in a linear and ascending map, but differs by a drawing to the center of both a simplified map and a balance of maps at a center point. It is a widening spiral rather than a lightning bolt or twisting path, but it can also be those in context if need be. Through the Cult of VIGEROS it offers another unique Serpent Path not on a tree, but rather in the stars and the reflection of those stars in the Underworld, reified in the center through a chiasmus much like sense data and neural impulses traversing the physiological pathways of the human brain. It puts the observer at the center of an annulus of selectable states of consciousness, affording scalable perspectives in holistic, particulate, and gestalt resolutions. It offers approaches of going below to rise above and "as above so below".

Dualism is a biologically and physiologically rooted evolutionary imperative in all sensate organisms, the driving program of survival in all species. At a cellular level it presents as the Pleasure Principle, that instinct of philia and phobia that draws organisms towards life-sustaining situations and repels them from exposure to harm and eventual death. The first recognizable dualism in biological consciousness then is Life and Death, in the experience of pleasure and pain. In the human organism this scales upwards through the reptilian, mammalian, and primate structures in the triune model of the human brain, and entails such things as the physiological necessities, libido, emotions, and social instincts. This is the stone sill of the narrow gate whose jams are Lust and Terror, and the amplified dualism of Life and Death seeping ever upwards from the cellular level to waking consciousness through the murky waters of the inner underworld.

Suffering is also rooted in biological precedents and likewise rises continually from our cells, organs, and cognitive structures into waking consciousness. Pleasure and pain are the resultant qualitative experiences of natural processes, the sum of wisdom of single-celled organisms exploded into scales that afford contemplation and self-reflection. It is in this scale that the trouble really begins I think. If we were single-celled organisms or less contemplative animals, the wisdom of the natural world would be closer to the surface. The Pleasure Principle or Fight or Flight Instinct would take us out of suffering a whole lot sooner. Pain and suffering are quite simply natural signals that something is wrong. The present human condition has programmed us to deny our pain and ignore our emotional and psychological suffering, to even take pills to numb us to the natural results of living out of balance with our own natures and the natural order of the manifest world. It has likewise made pleasure into a sin. We are lost in our so-called higher brains, intentionally conditioned, and habituated to contrived realities that any brainless protozoan would tell us, if it could only speak, will eventually result in our death and extinction.

The Garden of Bones is not some faraway place, nor is it only found in cemeteries and Charnal Houses. It is the soil under our feet, the minerals of our bones, the flesh of our parents' flesh, and the very atoms of our person. Our connections to the Ancestors exist in these selfsame substances. The memory of our entire line resides in the genetic helix of our DNA. The Akashic Record exists not only on the Astral, but in the collective human unconscious which may not be the same realms. As our will unfolds so does the Akashic Record and our connections to Theall and the Pleroma, including all that have lived before us and will live after us. By the stardust in our bodies and structures in our cells that may well prove to hold resonances with quantum levels of reality, we are also connected to even the most alien entities beyond our imaginations. We are all related.

The PAN-Aeonic Memeplex works as a map of consciousness; a developmental template; a curriculum of study; a manual for practice; a suite of modalities; a catalog of methodologies; a commentary and plan of human evolution; a cabinet of sympathies; a path of initiation; the aerospace-frame of a space-time vehicle suited for excursions into alien realms; a temple furnished for incursions from the daimonic underworlds; a holographic cartography center; and a communications array between endless numbers of worlds. The good Chronomage of Gallifrey only wishes he had such a reliable vehicle.

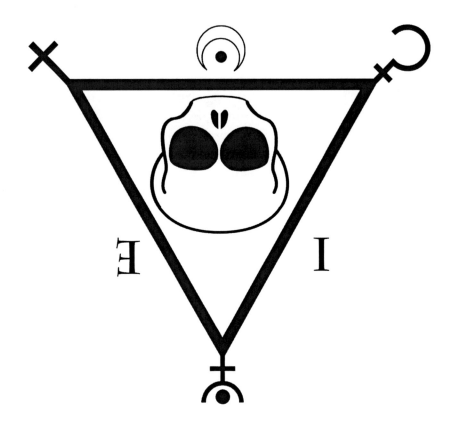

ΠΡΑΞΙΣ   PRAXIS

"Supplicant we stand before the Powers of Life and Death, and are heard of these Powers, and avail. Our way is the secret way, the unknown direction. Our way is the way of the serpent in the underbrush..." —Jack Parsons, "The Witchcraft"

The Witchcraft has ever known Death and that most intimately. Those that tread the Serpent Path have long seen beyond the pale, trafficked with the Shades of the Dead, and compacted with the citizens of Avernus and EREBOS. Like INANNA before them, they have delved the darkness and disrobed before ERESHKIGAL, and befriended Death in the in fathomable Ordeal. In the depths of the lightless pit, they have felt the caress of hell's own worm that dieth not and holds the unquenchable hidden fire, and found their truest selfnesses. What returns from the Charnal House returns with the seals and keys of the Underworld. It is not human in the common and pedestrian sense, but a true human being according to the ancient and natural order.

While magico-religious institutions may be characterized as "orthodoxies" and the various traditions of The Wicca as "orthopraxies", the work of Witchcraft seems best characterized as a heteropraxis personally tailored to individuals and small groups at local levels in their native landscapes. It is tailored also according to their truest natures and current best nurtures in study, practice, and state of awakening to Mystery. These of course can become concretized and codified into orthopraxic forms, but the moment they do not, all of their parts will perfectly fit the natures of those that come to engage them later, unless they are elastic and flexible. The natural tradeoffs between tradition and eclecticism should be obvious. I hold neither as any more valid than the other, but personally choose the latter according to my nature. Nature and nurture should be noted in the process of gaining skills in the Nameless Arte. Working with the Dead may prove harder for some than others, just as working with the Living.

Studying the literatures of science, magico-religion, comparative mythology, history, philosophy, psychology, anthropology, art and fiction surrounding Death, Dying, and the Dead is useful to our education. It is through cultivated literacy of the subject matter that we may learn a fuller spectrum of Death and the Dead in the human condition and unseen worlds. While this enterprise is able to provide interesting facts, such as the reality of coffin births and the use of corpse cages in attempts to thwart the return of the Dead, the fullness of our studies moves out of mere trivia only when we get our hands dirty.

The foundations for working with Death and Dead may be found in the simple choices and actions of daily life over time. Touching the Dead in every natural way possible brings a resonance with both Life and Death that cannot be obtained in any other way. Handling corpses, attending funerals, visiting cemeteries, acting as a pall bearer, grieving, attending to the grieving, sick, and dying are all invaluable life lessons. Contemplating where our food comes from and actually harvesting and preparing it can bring us to offer thanks to the lives of plants and animals extinguished in our own sustenance and survival. Slaughtering and cutting meat reveals the true nature of sacrifice. The fullness of Life cannot but bring us closer to Death and the Dead. Avoid neither for they both hold treasures.

Honoring the Dead in ritual acts at seasonal celebrations and additionally at specially appointed times throughout the year opens us to contact with the Spirits of the Dead. Ritual acts of respect for the Dead in our families, communities, and local landscapes are again invaluable life lessons, but they also put us at the threshold between the worlds and in contact with potential materials for stocking our cabinet of sympathies. The collection of flowers, earth and other materials at funerals, Day of the Dead and Samhain celebrations, and visits to sites associated with ancient ancestors can work on multiple levels, including the arcane materials used later in rituals beyond the celebratory.

Our Cabinet of Sympathies consists of those associations, lists and tables of correspondences, items, consumables, and substances that are intrinsic to our arte. It also consists of items cathexically invested with spiritual and emotional meaning. Everyone should read the literature and study the established correspondences in a variety of sources, but to be honest I use what works for me and skip the rest. I use what my Spirits have told me they like, what speaks to my own inner symbolic language, and what has proven effective over time. Not all of these sympathies match accepted conventions, and I really have no problem with that. Among the things that have proven invaluable in my work with Death and the Dead are as follows: Red Ochre; Myrrh; Frankincense; Copal, both black and white; Sage; Tobacco, including a nearly extinct species grown at a local historical site in their heirloom garden of plants cultivated by the Ancients; Corn Meal; Bread Crumbs; Blue Corn; food and drink items; material items I actually value and will miss in sacrifice; Animal Parts; Soil of a given origin I shall not name in print; items once belonging to departed loved ones; Dried Flowers collected from funerals; and any of a variety of tools and cathexic items useful to specific operations. As a matter of personal taboo and honor, I do not pour alcohol as libations on the Earth out of respect for Indigenous American Spirits of the Dead and those currently struggling with alcohol abuse.

Even if we do not actively believe in reincarnation, the act of attempting to remember past and future lives is a useful practice. If nothing else, it affords insights into your own imagination and inner worlds. Helping others do the same is equally rewarding. As noted earlier, I like to think of myself as the reincarnation of Allen Bennett. I really don't care how many others might also think of themselves likewise connected, or that hold me for a fool for thinking so myself. Other past life remembrances of note are an Egyptian Scribe and an adolescent Pictish boy killed by Vikings in a raid on his village. The latter was remembered in a sentence finishing session after an intimate ritual I shared with a coven-mate. He was the Viking that killed me, and no matter even if that experience was imagined, it afforded us a means to attend to our lingering differences.

Reading Omens, Portents, and Presages are staples of Witchery, as are Divination, Scrying, and various methods of Communicating with the Spirits. It is in my opinion that the term "Necromancy" best describes communicating with the Spirits of the Dead. Reading omens and receiving presages of upcoming departures of people we know and love is problematic enough to constitute a curse in my estimation. For a very long time I counted this among some the more debilitating curses that I carry, Deep Empathy being another. I simply had no idea what to do with such information and languished in torments over it for many years. For a long time, I alternately tried to deny my gift or struggled simply to cope with it with no help in sight. Eventually, I accepted it as a responsibility to prepare the way for my loved ones and help them from across the Veil. They have more than once returned those favors from their side of the fence by helping me. I have never told anyone that I saw an omen of their upcoming death. I have on occasion shared it with intimately trusted members of my magickal inner circle. People are sometimes frightened by this sort of thing, even magickal people, so I now share more sparingly.

Convoking with Death and the Dead and trafficking with the Spirits of the Underworlds is a matter again of nature and nurture. Not all techniques will work equally well for everyone, and it behooves us to explore as many as possible, or deign to fashion our own, if we intend to become conversant in the essences of Necromancy and the arte of diplomacy between the worlds. Before every ancient and elaborate technique is dug up and plundered in the search for knowledge, we should all consider the simple wisdom of just plainly and clearly talking to the Dead whenever and however we encounter them, and then just patiently and attentively listening with all our senses. Attending with keen awareness to our own oneiric adventures and active inner worlds is another important aspect of this simple wisdom.

As a matter of course in the unfolding of the promises of the Mage of Worms in the Gnosis and Convocations of our Angel-Daimons, we are afforded opportunities to enter into intimate relationships with Familiar Spirits. The term "my Spirits" as I use it entails Familiars, Helpers, Guides, Angels, Demons, Spirits of the Dead, and gods. In the matter of Familiars, whether Abremelinic or Sabbatic, the Shamanic undertones should be noted. Harking back to times before a third of the angels descended, Spirits of the Tripartite Shamanic Universe were the HGA's of practitioners. Those Spirits brought the visions of essential uniqueness to the human beings that forged compacts with them. For many today this has not changed. Some Familiars by their natures, like people, are better at working with the Dead. My own totem is populated with Spirits that resonate with my Scorpionic nature. Some of the more masterful ones are Owl, Crow, and Serpent, but Fox, Bear, Hawk and Heron also have something to offer in my work with the Dead.

Enlisting the Dead to our workings is a matter that I have held some ethical misgivings with, particularly according to the imperialistic methods of grimoiric tradition. I happen to think of the Spirits as persons, and I don't command, threaten, imprison, or enslave human beings out of my own nature. I actually adhere to the Silver Rule as much as possible, and this includes my interactions with the denizens of the unseen worlds, all of them, even the infernal and demonic. I use what I call "Martial Magick" on those Spirits that prove they do not hold the same ethics that I do. It is the same ethics I use with human beings that violate my will. In spite of my reluctance to use methods acceptable to some practitioners, I have in fact obtained the cooperation of the Dead in my workings. Among the most surprising allies I possess is a literal army of road kill. For probably twenty years I have uttered the words "go free, my relative" every single time I see a dead animal on the side of the road. The first time they came to my assistance was a tearful event because they communicated their gratitude to me.

Others may not agree, but among the more dangerous work with the Dead in which I have engaged seems to me to be acting as Psychopomp and Sin Eating; the latter I have only done once and suffered greatly for, even though it was for a loved one. Possession and offering a house for the Dead in our flesh are not so nearly as dangerous as the previous two, in my view. Some Spirits just don't want to be shown the door out of the Near Ethereal and have found for themselves techniques and non-human allies to affect that desire. Some are in the employ of or "worn" by non-human entities considerably more powerful and dangerous than suspected. Some departed Spirits are simply dangerous on their own. Some Spirits that seem to be disincarnate human beings actually turn out to be posing as the once-living for their own agendas. In any event the danger comes from protracted conflicts while unprepared, and unpleasant manifestations, including loss of life energy, physical and mental illness. Caution is strongly warranted.

Contemplating and meditating upon our own departure from the daylit world of the living is invaluably useful as is figuratively and ritually defleshing and vivisecting ourselves in the processes of Gnothi Seauton and Neti Neti. In preparation for the unfathomable Ordeal of coming to the gnosis of our truest selfness, a variety of well-known approaches and operations are available. Individual natures demonstrate that mileage will always vary in the use of technical arcane processes and rituals prepared by others. While the masters have left us paths to follow, the better ones in my opinion have insisted that we should cut our own paths through the jungle, and assured us that None may know the path by which we come to our own hidden gods. Not often enough noted, sometimes that includes us as a matter of the wholly unearned gifts of grace.

Spirit Gate Consecration Ritual

A ritual for the establishment of a Spirit Gate – A Spirit Gate may be used as a local entry point for Spirits of the Dead and Underworld, an exit in the work of acting as a Psychopomp to our own Dead, and a doorway for our own Sabbatic excursions. It draws inspirations from the Egyptian False Door, the "Gate of Death" of the Seductress of the Dead Sea Scrolls equated with LILITH, and naturally occurring Spirit Gates I have encountered in my landscape. I was first introduced to the practical efficacy of such constructed gateways by having to deal with one abandoned by another practitioner at the home of a lover. That the vector of this portal closely aligned with a naturally occurring gateway in her closet set up an unpleasant situation that looked in the Oneiric Realm something like a Spirit Highway over her home with an exit ramp to her closet.

I am not ashamed to say that what is presented here is not precisely how I created and feed my own Spirit Gate, but suggest that it will serve as a suitable basis for any creative or practiced occultist that wishes to utilize it in his/her own practices. Caution is warranted. Opening gateways for things we are unprepared to deal with can bring bad times, to say the least. Gates no longer in service should be ritually closed and earthed.

Location
A suitable location for a Spirit Gate is any two solid upright structures that look like jams in a doorway but are not part of a mundane door, gate, or archway that receives frequent foot traffic in the world of the living. Examples – a trellis arch in a location in a garden that is not often walked under, two poles erected for the purpose, trees, or an indentation in a structure that is not actually a doorway. Mine is constructed between two trees in front of my home in a location that people do not regularly walk.

Materials
Chosen ritual garb, tools, and auspicious times according to will, but night time seems to work best. Gather in advance two "firebrands". Two candles, torches, or lamps can stand in. Consumables needed are: Sage; Fumigation of Manna (Frankincense) & Copal (black for Death, white for the Dead); *Special Earth*; Water; Offerings of Food & Drink consistent with the number of Spirits called plus one for the Dead. A censor or small container, as well as self-lighting charcoals, are needed for your incense. Water is best brought to the site in a small corked bottle. The food offerings can be wrapped in crepe paper or cloth. If cloth is used, remove from the location afterwards. Toast with honey is sufficient for offerings, but bring what your Spirits require.

Preparations
A good working relationship with a Spirit of the Crossroads, Liminal Spaces, or Underworld is necessarily a pre-requisite of this sort of working. Gather materials well in advance and consecrate them to the specific use of the working. A singular portable kit makes for convenience. Insure via prolonged observation of your chosen location that you will not likely be disturbed during your work.

Temple
Lay out materials and chosen tools for convenience or auspicion according to will. Establish ritual space-time according to will.

Announce

"I am _____, come to this chosen place and time to establish a lasting gateway between the worlds of the Living and the Underworlds. I do this for and by my will as a diplomat between the worlds, and for the health of my people on both sides of the Veil. I shall faithfully attend to this gate and close it respectfully should I no longer require it."

Invoke

The following is an example only, use your own Spirits:

> "*IO, HEKATE! Mother of all Crossroads, Saffron-clad Queen of the Dead, First of all Witches which ruled before the gods of Olympus. Keeper of the Keys, Lighter of the Ways of the Underworld, Faithful Guide of the Path for lost PERSEPHONE. Invincible Titaness, Nocturnal One, Lover of Solitudes, I call your name for no idle purpose. I beseech thee attend unto these my rites. I call thee and adore thee. I call thee come; grace me with thy presence, thy favor and assistance. Come!*"

> "*Accept this humble offering, Ungirt One, Lady of Hounds.*"

Place your first offering.

Perform

Light and use the Sage to cleanse the periphery of the gate.

> "*By this smoke I prepare a gateway between the worlds.*"

Light the charcoal in your censor or container. Taking the Earth, outline the sill of the gate. Say:

> "*By this loam of the Earth, by the bones of my ancestors, by the bed of the ever-sleeping, I consecrate this gateway between the worlds.*"

Taking the bottle of water, outline the jams. Say:

> "*By this blood of the world, by this the elixir of Life and Death, I consecrate this gateway between the worlds.*"

Place Fumigation on charcoals. Light the Firebrands. Say:

> *"By this the light of the Keeper of the Ways of the Dead, and the Paths of the Underworlds, I establish this gate between the worlds."*

Wave the fire over the jams and upwards towards the lintel above your head. Place them at either side of the gate.

Taking the censor, outline the sill, jams, and lintel. Say:

> *"By this Fumigation I consecrate and establish this gateway between the worlds, by the power and favor of the Mother of the Underworld I make a Way for the Spirits."*

Projectively outline the gateway from left to right, then from right to left and lastly from the top of the lintel down the center, envisioning the split of a double door. Step forward and rend the Veil, open the doors outward towards you. "AShA!"

> *"I open the way between the worlds for my will and my work. AShA!"*

> *"Spirits of the Ancestors, I have opened a way! Spirits of the Dead, I have opened a way. Mother of the Underworld, I have opened a way. AShA!"*

Utter your own words of power. "AShA!" Make the sign of silence or a closing sign according to will.

> *"Ancestors, I bring you a gift."*

Place your last offering.

Thank the Spirits called in the rite, and offer license to depart.

Closing

Close temple according to will.

Collect your kit. Leave the Firebrands to go out on their own and collect later. Leave the door open.

Attendance and Upkeep

Watch the Spirit Gate and vicinity for activity. Make offerings to the Spirits at the Gate. Close the doors as needed. Deconstruct and earth the Gate if no longer needed, you move, or too much trouble comes through.

EPILOG

> *"Whatever you can do, or dream you can, begin it. Boldness has genius, power and magic in it."* —Goethe

I think of myself as no great magickian. My success-to-failure ratio is probably something approaching that of Edison with the light bulb and my inventions as equally "borrowed". I graciously acknowledge that just about whatever it is that I hold talents and learning in there is someone out there much better at it than me. The same is true for my natural endowments. I can at times be an oblivious fuckup, to be sure. What I don't capitulate to is that any of this means I have nothing worthwhile to say or share with the world. Some of that sharing is precisely the sort of fuckups that seem to me to be shared too infrequently in polite occult society.

While visiting a friend's house for the first time for an ecstatic drumming circle, I discovered a fascinating sculptural shrine on his property.

After many rounds of disappearing into the rhythms and chants of the circle, and much sacrament, I went off to water the woods. There in the darkness stood this roughly eight-foot-tall tower of bones in the dim moonlight. I was immediately seized by a presence and remembered in fact seeing this shrine in a dream. It held a message for me I was certain. I did my business and before leaving told it I would be back with an offering. When I returned with a handful of tobacco, I stood and soaked in the energy pouring off of it, told it I was there for a message like I saw in the dream, and called upon the name of THANATOS. I stood for a bit but nothing changed. There it was pouring out its cold and jittery energy, but no message. I thanked it and went back to the circle.

As oblivious as I can be sometimes what happened next is truly uncharacteristic of me, or I would like to think. The gathering that I was attending was at a place called Frog Holler on the leeward side of Peach Mountain. The presence of moonshine at these events is not at all unheard of, and I had just had some the last time I was out to Peach Mountain. A bottle was being passed and talked over. I reached for it, and it was handed to me amidst what I thought to be jokes about not drinking it. By this time I was quite inebriated, and it took what felt like an eternity to get the bottle open. I was going to be damned if anyone kept moonshine from me. As I do with moonshine I took about a quarter of a mouthful, swished, swallowed, and inhaled for the burn. It burnt just like the good stuff going down but had an awful aftertaste. I thought to myself that a lot of fuss had been made over of the worst batch of shine I'd ever tasted. I was prepared to tell my host just how much like ass his drink really tasted. It was then that it was brought to my attention that what I was holding was tiki torch fluid, again amidst much laughter. No one believed I had actually drunk any of it, and I had to assure them that I had. I also assured them that I was not going to die, that it was just like the snake handlers drinking strychnine. I washed it down with lots more beer and water, and a couple of hours later found I was surprisingly sober. The only ill-effect I noticed was an awful taste when I burped.

I chose to drive home. In route as the poison began to overtake me, I tried to recall what the poison control protocol was for petroleum items from my time as an EMT. I knew that it was either to induce vomiting or not induce vomiting—a 50-50 shot to get it right. Eventually I had to pull over to the side of the road as I was actually losing consciousness, burning up and sweating profusely, and convulsing. I got out of the van, and lay on the side of the highway thinking I would probably lose consciousness, aspirate on my own vomit, and die. I hoped that only someone would stop and save me. I decided I wouldn't vomit and that took all the strength I could muster. It was then that I got the message that I had made offerings for. It was something like this:

> "I'm Death, you dumbass! You don't fuck with me, and you don't fuck around with your life! Get up off your ass and live! Love the people you love with all your heart! The clan you're with is the one you've looked for over lifetimes. Do the things you have dreamed of doing! Take no care for how you will do them, just do them, because I can take you at any time and you'll never see me coming!"

Momentarily I came back around, shook violently in a cold sweat for a while and got in the van and started towards home again. Then it all dropped into my bowels like a lead hammer. I had to stop at a truck stop and profusely shit my guts out. That dirty bathroom smelled like a refinery when I was done. I feared someone would come in, light a cigarette and blow the place to pieces.

When I got home I called the Poison Control Center and got the skinny. The operator actually laughed when I answered her question about how I came to drink tiki torch fluid. Evidently hearing about moonshine was just too much for her composure. What I found out after all the laughing was that I had made the right call. Those that vomit most often die, or suffer such terrible lung damage simply from the fumes that they wish they had.

This was my third near-death experience. All of them have held meaningful messages and insights. It is also a running joke on Peach Mountain that dissolves into silent contemplation when I count coup on Death in the circle and recount the message I received. Then we go back to the sacrament, drinks and drums and laugh our asses off together. That I had a 50-50 shot at this big boner being laughed over at my wake is a fact that is not whatsoever lost on me.

AN OPEN LETTER PERTINENT TO THE SUBJECT MATTER

Beloved Souls on both sides of the Veil,

In the process of laboring over this essay on Death and the Dead, a person I have known for many years was killed in a car accident. She was a member of my partner's coven for many years, and a friend of the family for many years before that. I did not particularly like her, nor dislike her intently. She was a feature of my social landscape. She was a unique individual with strange quirks and habits. She made no qualms about being herself whether anyone liked it or not. We had our moments together, some laughter-filled, and some attended by harsh words.

She wasn't the sort to wear a seatbelt, nor was she the most attentive driver. The roads were icy that morning. Records show that she was on her cell phone not moments before the accident. She lost control of her jeep, it rolled, and she was ejected from the vehicle. She was killed instantly. Her five-year-old son survived the single-vehicle crash without injury, and remembers everything. His words in recounting what happened were these: "The car rolled, and Mommy flew out the roof and landed on the ground. They tried to wake her up, but she didn't wake up."

In spite of the fact that I didn't go out of my way to spend time with her, her departure from the world has touched me deeply. She will no longer be a feature of my social landscape in the daylit world, and yet she has returned to the fabric of unseen reality which I attend to most intently.

As much as Death and the Departed are features of Witchcraft and all traditions throughout history and around the world today, it is also an unavoidable feature of the mundane human condition.

Death is no respecter of persons. Death cares not what religion or magick you practice, if any at all. Death is a watchful and inevitable equalizer. Death brings the lofty down low and lifts up the downtrodden. None escape Death. None are untouched by Death. Death should be a constant reminder of our limited time here and an instigator to cherish every moment, no matter whom we are with or what we are doing.

In spite of the constant reminder of living fully that Death represents, most of us will be unaware of His shadow falling over us. We will marry and be given in marriage. We will eat, drink, and fuck, in abandon. We will revel together and sulk in loneliness. We will have children and raise them. We will run the rat race to survive and aspire to have more of all that is good. We will laugh and cry, and bitch and moan...and Death will take us all.

As a matter of my own personal taboos, I only speak the names of the close dead on special occasions. Old poets and occultists don't get that honor in my daily practices.

Jessica Howard, Asuka in your craft, first ancestor of Trinity of the Sacred Spiral Coven, go free my relative. Find the Summerland soon. Visit Lyric often and comfort him, for he will sorely miss you in his life…

NONE bequeaths Life,
LVX – Σκία – NOX – Εἴδωλο   Bradley Allen Bennett Two Crows

This work is one in a series which will further uncoil VIGEROS into the present space-time.

Bradley Allen Bennett considers himself a Dabblerist[CC] above any other magikal descriptor. What orders he may or may not hold membership in is secondary to his work, which is meant to speak for itself. He lives in rural southwestern Ohio with his little family, growing number of cats, and a host of unruly Spirits.

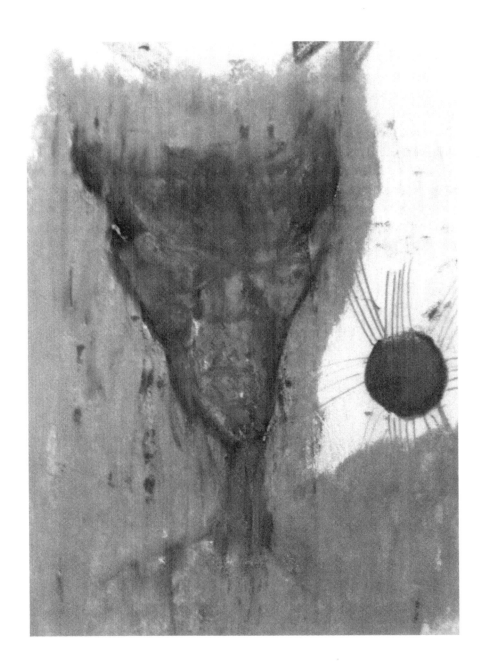

DEATH MAGIK AND THE PSYCHIC SPIRITUAL NATURE OF REVENGE

Dante Miel

L et us clarify something before we dig into this chapter. All of the nonsense that one reads and hears about in the fluffy, pompous and self-righteous diatribes of the Wiccan white light, new age, neo-pagan movement about whatever one does comes back to them threefold is a flat out lie and complete bullshit. There is zero evidence to support these outlandish claims. This threefold rule of witchcraft is an affront to any true magikian who is not afraid of their own true and complete nature, which includes their dark side. Nor is magik for those who are afraid to explore the realms of the shadow side of the human consciousness. Any and all attachment to religious death magik and the infernal-psyche-spiritual nature of the darkest most sinister side of ritual and ceremonial magik is presented here for informational and educational purposes only. Neither the author of this book, nor the publishers, or the editors, claim any responsibility as to the nature of this work, nor its contents, or any of the repercussions which may result from its usage. Death magik spells and rituals meant to bring about either the death or severe pain or sickness in another individual has many cross cultural references to the actual practices of such forms of magik.

The psyche-spiritual nature of revenge is based out of the rage of one's feelings towards another person, or persons, for acts that the magikian deems to be unethical and leaves one's self feeling wronged. Since there are no real legal definitions of metaphysical nor meta-magikal acts which result in the harm or death of another human being, it is incredibly difficult for a person to even hire a lawyer to take the magikian to court over such acts.

But each individual is fully responsible for looking into the legality of such actions in the law of their own country, state or province, etc.

The magikal practices and rites of self-initiation in this chapter, and indeed this entire book, draw upon many varied literary works from a multitude of cultures. Be they ancient, medieval, or of the aeonic stream of modern-day magik. The most popular aeonic current, within the modern day context of the occult theater is that of Aleister Crowley and the aeon of Thelema. The second aeon that followed that of Aleister Crowely's Thelemic current was the aeon of Maat, founded by Charles Stanfield Jones.

Black magik is most often confused with, or identified with, rituals and spells meant specifically to bring harm, bad luck, ill health, and even death to the receptor. Any form of magik is considered evil and the work of the devil in the eyes of devout Christians and other religious fundamentalist believers. This is pure bullshit. Certain precise techniques and philosophical approaches to magik contained in this book are black magik in the common sense of the term. They are created and carefully designed to align one's self with dark and infernal, vengeful and dangerous meta-magikal entities.

The true nature of black magik, how it differs from white magik, and even the beliefs and practices of common religions themselves has been dealt with elsewhere. Be they within the pages of this book or other scholarly and literary works written by students of religion, philosophy, and even magik itself. To follow through with a spell meant to cause harm or, even more intensely, that of death magik itself weighs upon the soul. Magik meant to specifically bring about the death of another human being, to an enemy, is not to be taken lightly in any way, shape, or form. These are ritual acts of magik and spells specifically meant to ruin other peoples' lives, by means of harm, illness, and even death. As far as common law is concerned, it is difficult to prosecute a person for casting a ritual spell that results in the injury or death of another human being. This does not, however, mean that the magikian is completely free of repercussions from such ritual acts and spells. Bring about a fundamental shift from within one's own psyche, and that very same psyche will, by default, bring about a fundamental shift in one's self-awareness and cosmic, psyche-sexual-meta-magikal nature.

As with any form of magik, one must have a complete and solid grasp of the nature of the workings, but also a firm understanding of one's own ability and commitment to the rituals and spells. The magikian must, as a rule, be willing to take full responsibility for any outcome, which may result from such forms of dark, harmful magik—especially when it comes to death magik. If the magikian isn't 100% clear with their intent and objective, harm or death may fall upon other people not specifically meant to be pulled into the magikal vortex created. There are stories floating around, whereby a family member or loved one is struck down and killed or permanently injured because the magikian was not 100% clear on the nature of the desired outcome of the curse.

Some of the rituals and spells contained in this chapter are not to be taken lightly at all, especially those rites involving the Petro Voudon spirits. They require blood. It is imperative that you, the magikian, take full responsibility for your actions. Spirits requiring blood, and freshly drawn blood at that, will bring great misfortune and horribly terrifying, vivid nightmares for longer than what most people can handle. Unless you are willing to take all of this on, I strongly suggest that you first seek out a true Voundon Priest or Priestess before following through with any of these rites or rituals.

The Voudon rites contained in this chapter are all based on the Petro rites, and upon the more intense and even more dangerous rites of Palo Mayombe. It is the responsibility of the author and publishers to give good and fair warning not to perform these rites without first consulting a true and bonafide Palero or Petro Voudonist. WHY?

Death magik is not anything to take lightly, in any way, shape, or form. Death magik implicitly implies that one is both willing and desiring to kill another human being. Point blank...this is heavy shit. Be willing to sacrifice your own well-being, and possibly your own life, which may happen if for any reason any of the rites, rituals, or spells backfire. Basically, do not do this unless you are completely and fully willing to face these consequences.

This is purely for informational and educational purposes only. As a side note, it is very unlikely that any of these spells or rituals will work for the neophyte or novice practitioner, nor for those who are not entirely one hundred percent sure or completely dedicated. The rites, rituals, spells, and tribulations contained in this chapter are all explicitly the darkest and blackest of all forms of magik. The spirit seals and sigils, or "veves" as they are known in Haiti, are mainly dangerous spirits to work with. Some of the other forms or ceremonial functions contained in this chapter are based on the Ancient Greek Magical Papyri, Greek and Roman binding spells and curses, and have been adapted to suit the functions of this study from the works of

Steven Flowers' *Hermetic Magic*. To the initiated, the similarities between these forms of magik will be clear.

There are two distinct streams of the Hermetic tradition as it functions in the world today, both of which have their origins dating back to antiquity. The first of which is the philosophical stream as contained in the Hermetical literature, most of which dates back to the medieval era, and is exemplified in the somewhat contradictory and at times made up ceremonial magikal rites of groups, such as the various groups claiming to be the true repository of Hermeticism. This is not of any real concern to the pragmatic and post-modern Typhonian magikian. What is of significance to the actual practicing magikian is to get a firm grasp on the actual form and function of this form of pragmatic hermetical magik. Once one has done the self-initiations into the true Typhonian form of magikal operations, then they are able to adapt *The Greek Magical Papyri in Translation* (see Hans Detier Betz) to suit their own intuitive needs.

The self-initiations of ancient Greeks and Romans, and the true original stream of Hermetic magik, will be extrapolated upon within the context of the practicing magikian as opposed to a strictly scholarly one. For the most scholarly work on the true Hermetic path as practiced by the ancients, I refer the sincere student firstly to Steven Flowers' *Hermetic Magic* and Don Webb's *The Seven Faces of Darkness* for insight into the Typhonian Hermetic magikal current. For a strictly historical collection of the actual ancient Greek and Roman tradition, I refer the student to *The Greek Magical Papyri in Translation* by Hans Dieter Betz, and *Curse Tablets and Binding Spells of the Ancient World* by John G. Gager.

Firstly, let us begin with the self-initiation rites into the true ancient magikal Typhonian current as is updated for the modern-day magikian. The hermetic tradition has two separate modern-day versions. One is that of the philosophical branch, upon which the Hermetic Order of the Golden Dawn and other modern-day magikians focused upon. This Order was a hodge-podge of separate systems, which at times was more confused than direct. Then there exists the actual pragmatic and practicing branch of the true ancient Typhonian branch of Hermetic magik. Now let us get into the actual nature of the Typhonian pragmatic current.

For this you will need one special ceremonial stone, four red bricks, and a sheet of genuine papyrus or true parchment paper. If these are not available, try to get some paper made of the palm tree, or other form of handmade paper, as these will suffice. Black and red inks will be necessary. For 'Ink of Black Magik', India ink will suffice along with the addition of crushed blueberries and blackberries and with drops of your own blood added to forge a connection between you and the ink. Next, you will need to make the 'Ink of Typhon'. Take up red berries and a pomegranate, and soak these ingredients together with cooked artichoke and mashed up purple figs. Add several drops of your own blood to this concoction, and then strain out all of the solids. The amounts of each individual ingredient will have to be felt out and brought to your own desired darkened blood-reddish color. If you are going to be doing this with or for a woman, then have her add some of her own menstrual blood to the ink. Store each individual ink inside its own small glass jar that is as air tight as possible. Mark each individual ink as thus. Make sure to use only fine camel or horsehair paintbrushes or a real feathered pen and quill.

Take red bricks and place them together, carefully placed side by side as to form a basic altar. This is the basis of your true ancient Hermetic Typhonian altar. Have at your disposal a fresh red onion, sheet of papyrus or natural paper as described before, and a thin, small piece of flexible sheet metal, and a stylus for engraving into the sheet metal. Gather dried grass or fresh grass and allow it to dry completely. Also gather a small amount of clay along with nails and sturdy, yet thin twine. You can use cloth, a sewing pin, and twine instead if that is your preference. These are the makings of a binding spell based on the ancient Greco-Roman tradition. It is always best to bathe just prior to any rite that you are going to take seriously.

Carefully lay out a black cloth upon the floor. Place the red bricks side by side in the center. Burn black and red candles for light. Make sure that there are no electrical distractions, such as the sound of telephones or cell phones ringing, refrigerators humming, or other electrical noises. Be sure to turn off all electric lights. Have all the necessary ritual items close at hand. Be clothed in clean black liniments or robe. Pace upon the alter a representation of Typhon-Set. Inscribe upon the thin piece of sheet metal as explicitly as you can your intentions, and give thanks and blessings to Typhon-Set. Wipe it with the inks and roll up the metal, and then seal it by pouring upon it both black and red wax while calling out your will to Typhon-Set. Set it upon the altar. Burn incense of spices, frankincense and myrrh. Pass the rolled-up metal binding spell or curse spell through the smoke of the burning incense.

Next, take up thy papyrus (or other natural paper substance) and carefully write out the precise desired outcome of the magikal working with the inks that you made. Be sure to give thanks and to call upon the energies of Typhon-Set and paint their names upon the paper, along with the curse or binding spell. Take up the clay and form out of it a replica of the intended victim with their arms and legs bound together with the twine. Impale the nails into the body where you want the pain inflicted. Wrap this up inside of the metal curse tablet. Or do the same with a small figurine made out of fabric and stuffed with straw or dead grass.

With a piece of the papyri paper, write the spell again. Slice an opening into the red onion, fold up the curse/spell and carefully insert it within the onion. Drip black and red wax upon these, bury them outside beneath the dirt during either the full or waning moon and demand that the spirits of nature devour these items just as the natural world, and Typhon-Set will bring about the curse or binding spell into being. Be sure to give sincere thanks unto Typhon-Set and to all of the nature spirits helping you to carry this curse through until its end.

Finish up by giving utmost gracious thanks to the Beings and Spirits, who assisted you and will see the curse through. Then put the bricks away out of sight for another time, carefully wrap up the black cloth and all other materials and place them someplace safe where no one else will see or touch them.

POINTING THE BONE

This is strictly for information and educational purposes only. Neither the author nor the publisher can be held accountable for any actions that any individuals may take based upon the information in this essay.

Pointing the bone or bone pointing, as it is also called, is an Australian Aboriginal death curse ritual. It is believed to never fail. Western perspectives on the occurrence of death as a result of this ritual consider it to be, when effective, brought upon by the victim psychosomatically. More often than not the bone used is a human bone but can be a kangaroo bone or even a piece of wood.

Strands of human hair are inserted into a hole in the back of the bone and sealed in place with natural plant resin. This bone is then charged with intense psychic energies and ritually consecrated. During the actual cursing, the bone is pointed directly at the targeted victim, and the sorcerer's will-power is forcefully projected through the bone to strike at them.

My own variation on this curse ritual is to carve an opening in the back side of a straight length of human bone (arm, leg, or finger bone), or alternately an animal leg bone, and hallow it out. Carve a small hole in the opposite end that is just big enough for powder to be blown through it.

In a small container blend together a mix of human or animal bone powder, finely ground herbs and poisonous plants. Grind up dried venomous spiders or scorpions and blend this into the powder. Alternately, you can use the potion of venomous arachnids and serpents and sprinkle some of these into the powder. Let this dry out completely. Write the name of the targeted victim onto a small piece of paper. Light a red or black candle and ignite this piece of paper. Be sure to carefully capture all of the ashes and blend them into the powder. Carefully pack this powder into the hallow bone making sure to not allow any of it to pour out of the small hole in the front tip. The stem of a feather can be used to plug the front opening. Close up the back end of the bone with natural plant or tree resin, or some other method or materials can be used as well.

Handle this bone carefully so as to not allow any of the contents inside of it to empty out. When the time comes, you can use this bone to both poison the individual and perform the 'bone pointing'. Remove the feather or other material on the front tip, point the bone at the target victim and project the full force of your willpower at them as you blow the contents of the bone in their direction. If you are brave enough and not concerned with any legal repercussions, you can blow the entire contents of the bone directly in the victim's face. You can use your imagination to realize the kind of affects this can have upon the victim.

A/P TUBAL+CAIN

-Seven Feet Under-
The Heart of Fire beneath the Tongue of Silence

Kyle Fite

The Lord of Illusion is The Lord of Life.
The Lord of Reality is The Lord of Death.
In Truth, these Two are the Same Lord
And Never Divided.

T he Magician is etymologically a Manipulator of Maya, one who is not subject to the Laws of an Illusory Universe but rather a Master of them. He is the Millstone and not the Grain. As such, he operates on the periphery of average human experience while shifting the same with aid of an arte incomprehensible to the materialistic mind. It is a romantic picture and one which is easily misunderstood if these factors of Illusion and Power are viewed through the limited lens of Life. Without equally entering an awareness of Death, the Magician can have no contact with the Reality empowering his creative usage of Illusion. To simply conceive of this "Otherworld" is not enough. One must link it to Life through the vehicle of one's Experiential Entity. This link is the result of a Deep Initiation, and one which will forever transmute the Vehicle through which it is accomplished.

Life and Death are often polarized via an inherited Aristotelian Logic. Either a thing is "Alive" or a thing is "Dead." It cannot be both. As Life is understood as possessing certain qualities (such as activity, awareness, growth and so forth), Death is defined by the opposite characteristics. This creates a problem in that Death is being viewed from the standpoint—and logic—of Life. One can only presume that these imagined qualities (or anti-qualities) have some sort of reality. In other words, one is applying a simple formula based on assumption, the same being born of very restricted experiential capabilities. An example would be the acceptance that "grass is green." It is how it appears to you and how it seems to appear to everyone else. The type of perceiving/categorizing faculty at work here has also been known as crucial to one's simple survival in the material realm. Through various symbolic signals, one takes courses of action which benefit the player in the human game. Logic, experience and hard-wired biological impulse all conspire to justify the conclusion "grass is green."

As we learn more of the natural world, however, we soon discover that there is no inherent or absolute "color" in the phenomena we observe as grass. We then accept the experience in context of concepts which are simply extensions of the initial logic, experience and impulse. The means by which we determined that "grass is green" are the means which determine that "grass is NOT green." Regardless of viewpoint, the "is/is not" dichotomy prevails, the Aristotelian Law of Non-Contradiction. And this extends into our understanding of *all* phenomena, including what it means to be alive or dead.

From this dualistic perceptive habit, we make an assumption and react to it. Whether one embraces the idea of an afterlife or infinite oblivion, one is left to interface with reality through the tools of engagement at one's disposal.

We observe many purporting to know this or that about death and what awaits the human entity who has succumbed to biological terminus. Even if we hold specific religious views on the matter, we are inclined to discount the similar views of others which do not fit our theological framework (again, the Law of Non-Contradiction is clung to). Thus, the Christian is suspicious of the Muslim account of the afterlife, even while both profess certainty of the same.

The question, then, is WHAT can we TRULY know of Death while Living? And HOW do we even begin to explore this realm which seems to be entered only by the sacrifice of the self which seeks it?

Our model for this process is that of Esoteric Freemasonry which carries through its Rite a condensation of Initiatic Teaching from far older cultures. The symbols and "working tools" gathered along the way all serve to support the great climax of the ceremony: the Death and Resurrection of Hiram Ab-iff, Master Builder and Heir of the Magical Metallurgist, Tubal Cain.

***

There are times in this human life when we may find ourselves desirous of death. Folding to frustration, weariness or despair, we conceive of comfort in the covering of our casket with a cold clod, the silence of the grave hush-ing some unbearable assault upon our psyche. Whether this closing of the curtain opens to a calming cloudscape past pearled gates or simply signi-fies the closure of consciousness with cessation of brain-waves, we expect a "break."

This hope is well played by opportunists from every religious angle. In-troducing the idea of Hell (or at least tough transitions best avoided) keeps the Ultimate Sabbath from being a Workweek Guarantee. Conditions must be fulfilled in the eyes of one's "Employer" unless one wants to keep "work-ing through the weekend" at a hated job.

Control thereby gains a sales pitch as it sells Spiritual Insurance.

"If you want your respite, do THIS (read: PAY UP-in coinage, obedi-ence, societal support). Otherwise…" (Father Pharisee whistles and shakes his head).

This isn't religion. It's a ploy.

No human being holds the Keys to your Beyond. The game is old and, if we ascribe to anything approximating Crowley's Aeon of Horus, the game is DONE.

Death is not a shadow looming over our mortal lives. It is an element twisted and fused into a Life of which we are part.

Likewise is this Life wrapped into every fiber of Death. This gives rise to the Death Fetishists who obsess—through the portals of their organic lives—over transcendental ecstasies found through the extremities of sun-dry "sorcerous artes," duly dressed in gothic garb, necromantic ornament and alterations in the experience of the bio-machine. On one hand, this is a natural inclination at a certain stage of awakening. On the other, it is a retardation of a process which must not be halted half-way.

Life and Death are not themselves Absolutes. They are two faces of one coin. We do not pit Light against Darkness. These two reveal each other, opening a means to grasp—if in part—the Reality which gives rise to both.

***

I do not desire Stasis. Heaven's Harp and Atheistic Anesthesia both raise suspicion in my soul. What might be an alternative to such views?

I am reminded of Resurrected Lazarus in the once controversial and now-forgotten film *The Last Temptation of Christ*. Before he meets an assassin's blade, his killers had to ask what it was like on the other side.

He replies that it was really no different than it is HERE.

This was NOT the answer they were expecting—and it made the knife-plunge all the more easy.

We cannot accept the placid heaven of the eternally obedient sheep or the simple snuff-out of those who can see no further than their material experience. But we also hunger for something beyond what we KNOW. Sometimes we are motivated by a desire to quell fear or uncertainty. But even when this has been put aside, there is an energetic drive, a curiosity and need, which propels us onwards.

As long as we remain in light, we are magnetized towards the darkness. This darkness, however, does not conclude the matter. Rather, it is driven back towards the light.

We are going into the Night to return to Dawn. It is through this exchange that we can become more than we are. The Thesis of Hegel leads us to Antithesis—and this propels our hungry soul towards Synthesis, the New Thesis, and the Next Rung on the Ladder ascending to Distant Stars.

***

There was a day in my life when I felt my heart seize up in my chest. I literally fell down upon the stairs and truly believed: This is IT! The END! BIO SHUTDOWN!

As sweat gushed from my face, my step-daughter appeared. I told her I thought I was dying and get ready to call 911. She looked at me and said I was being dramatic and faking. She walked away.

I felt utterly alone in that moment. I was going to DIE and there was no help.

My body then began to FREEZE. I was shaking with hypothermia. I couldn't move save for shivering.

And then…the ice began to turn to FIRE. I was cooking from the inside out. I can't describe the pain. It was as if I was being microwaved. I'd later read of these two elemental passages in the Tibetan Book of the Dead.

It was in that moment that I felt my heart cry out:

Not here! Not NOW!

I was hanging on some World Tree and gushing anything but glamour. I wasn't thinking of "Death Mysteries" or Runes…I was giving every atom of my being to holding onto this human life where I was yet needed. How would my little son go on without his Dad? What of those who depend upon and need me? What of all I have yet to learn, to know, to enter? I felt something of what Jack Parsons expressed with his final words:

"I'm not DONE yet…"

I don't feel that I WILLED myself back to life. Rather, I was given an Opportunity. I was touched by the Hand of Grace and Vitality. About to evaporate, I slid back into my Urthlife.

But I DID see something on the Other Side of that Gate, something I wish to SHARE.

We humans are joined through our mortality. It is to this reality I speak, the strange paradox of temporal life active within eternal space. I know many who peruse these words will never know me aside from these few words printed on paper. Divested of skin, bones buried in some unmarked grave, I extend my hand from another realm to speak to the yet living. What I offer are symbols and suggestions which may serve idea and imagination as these rise through human consciousness to reach beyond it.

**

The Brother of Osiris truly became such only after he had sliced his sibling into pieces, placing each at a precise location within the Great River, the Nile. Fourteen were the parts, one for each Day—and Night—linking Sabbaths (or SUN-Days). Often treated as treachery, the Work of Set was an Initiatory Action. On one hand, we find a parallel to the bloody betrayals of the Three Ruffians in Masonic Lore, those uninitiated ones who slashed the Master Builder into his Grave. On the other, we have the Brothers of the Lodge *behind* these figures, bringing the Candidate to the "Rubbish of the Temple" where the Mystery of the Resurrection can be given expression.

Students of Esoteric Masonry will know that the Villains, pernicious as they may seem, embody the Mystery of the Lost Word, a Mystery which will only be given to the "Raised Master Mason" in Symbolic (or "Substitute")

Form. The Slayers and the Slayed are One Thing, divided for "Love's Sake" and united through that same Power. Each Killer will suffer the Fate of Hiram, thus uniting with him through Karma. Hiram's rebirth (from three auspicious wounds) will likewise serve as the Redemption of the Ruffians.

Note that each one of these murderers' names begins with a "J" (or "Yod"). Qabalistically, this letter has the numeric value of "5." 5 times 3 is 15, the number of the Devil Card in the Tarot (Set—or Satan). We find here that Osiris will rise from Death as the Redeemer of Set. If we wish to compare mythologies, we see that Jesus is the Redeemer of Satan (an idea we encounter in the Mythos of William Blake). This Redemption is more than a simple act of forgiveness—it is an Alchemical Process, the energetic exchanges of which are merely typified in Masonic ceremony.

The most sincere and spirit-driven aspirant enters the Temple in Search of LIGHT. To TRULY come into this Gnosis, the "Darkness" must be clarified. The most effective of initiatory rites will strip away all that keeps this Darkness beneath the skin. It has been written that Osiris is a "Black God," and this must be realized in the total consciousness of the candidate before the Grave can be entered—and departed from!

***

MAHABONE!

Upon the first utterance of this strange word at the climax of the Masonic Rite, the Newly-Raised Master Mason tends to be struck by one association: the familiar word BONE.

It's enough.

There are many commentaries on this odd word which is often interpreted as meaning "The Builder is Dead!" But this hardly expresses the fact that the Builder has, in fact, RISEN.

Masonic Scholar Albert Mackey makes the observation that the correct word is composed of not 3 but 4 syllables. Bear in mind that the Lodge room (itself a Living Symbol) has three officers but FOUR WALLS, the North being that "Place of Darkness." It is this Darkness which must fuse with a Triune Life ere the two may become one.

Within Masonry's eclectic heritage of diverse cultures, we may see "Maha" as that prefix indicating the "Great" or "Supreme." The "Great Bone" is the Skull, a symbol commonly connected to Masonic Ritual. This symbol, however, holds more meaning than most people (and even Masons) will consider.

At the beginning of one's Masonic voyage, the skull is a symbol of mortality, the Mason being earnestly encouraged to contemplate it as a symbol of all things coming to pass. At the end of the Rite, it is seen as "that which remains," the permanent portion of flesh life. It joins with the Acacia—or Evergreen—as a symbol of continuance. There are both moral and metaphysical implications here.

In the end, the 3 Degrees of Masonry are sewn together through a 4th Power. Rebirth is not as the return of Lazarus to the Land of the Living. It is entry into a Different Dimension, the powers of which will be carried into one's temporal life.

***

There are no ghastly skeletons to haunt us. We carry one inside our own flesh.

I look in the mirror and fix my hair (what's left of it). I catch those lines cut into my face by time and turn to see which side really IS "best." I smile at myself and wonder if I still have "the charm." And the mirror starts going all Dorian Grey...

I can see it, the "Skull Beneath The Skin." I could put an incision into my face and then pull it off—but there's no need. What lies beneath the muscle and meat is right there, peering out from the pores. My own personal Grim Reaper. I clack teeth and pull my lips back. There's his mouth. My tongue dissolves with my larynx. Do I wish they'd have stayed? Without the windpipe and lungs, they're pretty worthless—and I no longer have either.

I beat out a cry for help on my xylophone ribcage. Morse code begins to take on a congo beat. Talkin' Effluvia Blues No. 33. Someone grabs my hand and my fingers slide right off.

My face falls off the chin and lands in the bathroom sink, clogging the drain. No way I'm going to work today. I'd call an ambulance but my jawbone just hit the floor. I reach down, thinking, "Samson could kick some ass with this thing" when everything just crashes onto the tile like a child's building blocks.

WAKE UP!
WHY DON'T YOU PUT ON A LITTLE MAKE-UP???

Hiram help me, I'm drag-queening my way down the Via Dolorosa. I'm hexagrammed in The Tomb, gelatinized and 100% FUBAR.

Then here comes THE LION! It starts as a gurgle in the sink, sizzling my rumpled grimace. The whole thing blows to pieces and water is spraying everywhere. But FIRE is putting it out as steam hisses and paint begins to blister from the walls! Between FUCK YOU and MARRY ME, some God grabs my wrist and hauls me up from Hell.

***

Winking and Blinking, I'm but a beaked-babe crushed into a noetic nest. Even after I've taken flight and made my first kill, I have no idea that creatures on the Terran Plane will set up temples to venerate me.

They confuse Noesis for Gnosis!

Soon I will have no care for their "Because." I destroy their Gods, and they grasp at my wings to set me up in the Place of their Void.

I have no Mystic Maxim to give. My neck lengthens, and I become the Vulture, hungry for carrion.

Here is the deal, raw and real:

If you can read these words, you are in the Urthzone. This essay is directed only at the Urthbound. It is a message sent from a distant Planetary System (you'll find out soon enough which one).

Please know: this document will self-destruct in…

…what does it matter?

The Supernova of your Sunshine is inevitable and, ergo, imminent. This is an important point: the Inevitable is Imminent. So much of your Human Culture is based upon Denial of this FACT.

The equation "Inevitability = Imminence" disconnects your flesh from bone. What woman with drooping tits will choose kneecaps vs. promise of perk? What letter-jacket will pick the whimpering worm over the homecoming cockstand?

Breast-tape and hair-dye for men. A whole generation turns go-carts from the headstone on the track. Drugs, lotions and potions. We are embalming ourselves in denial!

But we feel some deep anger, some holy hatred, some monstrous love. We turn it around and drive against the flight-fleet. We drive straight into the Mouth of our own Mortality!

Silver coins spray from our palms, and we are crucified one way or another.

Wounded by the Gar given to Odin, we PLUMMET.

We leapt to get into the womb of the mother, and we leap again to enter the womb of Space!

Some call this demise.

We call it "Leveling Up."

The Master Builder, Hiram Abiff, oversaw the building of King Solomon's Temple. The plans for this edifice were given directly to Solomon by God Almighty and Hiram was the Hired Technician. There was, however, an element which Hiram brought to the table, an addition not part of Solomon's vision. This was a work called THE MOLTEN SEA.

The Molten Sea was a manifestation of the Genius of Tubal-Cain, of Hephaestus. Within the Temple of Solomon, this would serve as a communion between Cain and Abel. Darkness and Light would be joined via the great Pillars of Boaz and Jachin. The Shekinah known as the High Priestess would, at last, become ISIS UNVEILED.

This never came to pass. Treachery in the Temple resulted in Water being added, prematurely, to the Molten Sea. This disrupted the alchemical process and caused a chemical combustion. This betrayal has been played out time and again through history. Just as genius is about to place the capstone on the Royal Arch, the Traitor appears. From John Wilkes Booth to those who set up Jack Parsons, we find the Molten Sea defied. They are afraid of the inevitable.

But we know the Inevitable is the IMMINENT, even as both serve what we seek: IMMANENCE!

**

There are some who would decry Christ Crucified. These are ignorant for Christ is Crucified Daily. The Transubstantiation of the Catholic Mass is merely a MIRROR reflecting the Reality.

When Jesus died, the Temple Veil was rent in twain!

When the Molten Sea was sabotaged, the EARTH Itself was torn asunder and Hiram Abiff entered the loins of the Great Mother.

Hiram plummeted through the Nine Strata of Earth to reach the Source of his personal vision, the flaming Planetary Core! It was within this Temple of FIRE that he received the TRUE WORD of the MASTER MASON. Ascending through the same nine strata, we find the Master Builder emerging.

These nine strata are a numeric variant on the primordial SEVEN GATES. Plunging through 7 and emerging from 7, the Master Mason is exposed to FOURTEEN POINTS.

Ergo, Hiram comes forth dazzling in the Gnosis of Osiris assembled!

Let us remember, the phallus of Osiris was not found. Isis fashioned a new phallus from clay, and it was from this member that she conceived the child Horus.

14 parts + 1 (Phallus) = 15, (again) the number of the Devil Card of the Tarot, Capricorn, PAN, the ALL.

15 = 1 + 5 = 6, the Holy Hexagram, Man and God joined via the Masonic Square and Compasses (Terrestrial and Celestial Measurement).

This is not symbolic abstraction. These are symbols reflecting YOUR LIFE.

The fleshly phallus of Osiris was the means of physical generation and sexual ecstasy. When Isis created the new phallus, she fashioned a means of spiritual generation and Gnosis.

***

I have taken men down to their deaths. I was wearing a black suit and hard shoes, poised on red carpet and present in the Master Mason Ceremony. I drew my hand across the human breast and cut the heart. I wanted the death to be felt as real, complete. When the body was severed from soul, we could then bring the soul into its own space. This is emphatically NOT a dualistic action. The soul, truly awakened, may reincarnate into its own flesh, at last one with it!

The Flesh face will hold to the human skull as Deathgate symbol. The Skullsoul will wear a different icon about its crumbling clavicles. Organic and Prismatic, this Jewel cannot be ossified in Time. It is the Jewel of the Master in the East. It is the Vehicle of the Rising Fire.

We bring the Candidate into Death that Death may lunge forward into Life from its Spiritual Synthesis!

If this doesn't happen, we will report, as did Lazarus, that everything just continued on. The Hells and Heavens we have conceived have all been known on earth. There is no secret invention of an imaginary devil waiting to outdo what we have done to one another. We move from the ice and fire of the stairs where I began to melt into the Tibetan Bardos. Here Karmas do not function in the Kindergarten way we imagine. We undergo the "walk." Qlipoth don't gratify Lovecraftian leanings. We come face to face with shame and regret even as we find our prime components exposed. At any second, we're about to be sucked down the hall of Yellow Light. The murderer relives his father brushing aside a drawing in crayon and retreats to the womb.

House, Sun and Family are destined to be drawn again.

OTOA PUBLIC PAPER:
THE MISTAKE OF THE MEONISTES

"Meon" is a word often connected with the work of OTOA-LCN through the writings of Michael Paul Bertiaux. It is a realm (if we can call it that) which has been described as an "icy nothingness." But truly, the Meon is no more "icy" than it is "fiery." These words (in fact, ALL WORDS) derive from an experience which is Non-Meonic. They are simply deemed as useful in a Wittgensteinian "pointing" at something which operates outside the linguistic level of consciousness. Even *these* words are "false" for they imply that the Meon is a thing (i.e. something which exists). Language is tricky like that. Even if we say the Meon does not exist and is not in any way a thing, we have made it such by simply NAMING IT.

At this point, we may well be thinking of our friend, Lao Tzu with his "Tao that cannot be named." Wittgenstein said that "Whereof one cannot speak, thereof one must be silent." As Esoteric Engineers, however, we do not feel that the present limits of our technologies (including language) need be settled for. Wittgenstein also spoke of climbing a ladder only to throw it away when we had transcended its reach. Jacob's ladder witnessed angelic beings (Loa) both ascending *and* descending. If language is the ladder, we feel we might do better than ditching it—or crashing down the stairs and breaking a neck.

Language is an expression of Maya, Illusion, the World of Duality. But the Magician is, by definition, a Master of Maya. We do not seek some one-way street to a Nirvanic White-Out. There is a glorious pouring back and forth of the Waters in the Aquarian Tarot Card called The Star. This Water is the result of Fire and Ice colliding at the Crossroads where Eternity and Temporality meet. This is not meant to be a poetic statement but a technical observation. Eternity can only be such through this interface. Otherwise, it falls from itself into the occlusion of linguistic limits. To speak of the Eternal, the Infinite, the Void is to act as Blake's Urizen and encompass the illimitable. This must always bind us within a circle and keep us from that which we have sought to know.

We know many students of this work have desired to know the Meon, for it is suggested as a verity "Beyond." The Inner Fire longs for its Home and rages against all cages. "The Meon," therefore, appears as a Bull's Eye to we might Hat Trick. It is not THIS so it must be THAT.

But the MEON is neither THIS nor THAT.

Ice is a symbol of stasis contrasted with the wild growth of the warm seasons. But we know that ice is active, vital and alive. We call the Meon "Icy," and yet it is on the other side of Ice. It is on the other side of FIRE.

The MEON is partner to the Pleroma. Pleroma is the FULLNESS, and MEON is the EMPTINESS.

In our teachings, we draw a distinct line between the "Meontologists" and the "Meonistes." The Meon isn't "evil," but the Path of the Meonistes IS. These are those who would sacrifice Pleroma for Meon. Pleroma exists by means of the Meon, and Meon has its Reality (we cannot say "Being") via Pleroma. But the Meonistes are polarized into a Darkness which defies both Pleroma and the Love of Pleroma-Meon.

In essence, if you think "entering the Meon" is taking some daydream headtrip into an Astral Antarctica, you have missed the boat. In Hebrew, Meon means DWELLING. It is the SPACE (UNSPACE) in which MANIFESTATION can MOVE.

Please consider the relation between the Gnostic Meon and the Buddhist "Luminous Void."

Are these the same thing?

Now, consider the difference between "Bodhisattva" and "Buddha." "Buddha," as such, has entered Nirvana. The "Bodhisattva," on the other hand, has rejected Nirvana and bound himself to Spacetime until ALL BEINGS achieve LIBERTY (Enlightenment).

Is the Bodhisattva a Buddha?

We propose this:

The Meonistes are seeking Buddhahood through Desire for Nirvana. Despite their efforts, they can never enter but fall into one of the Bardo Zones, again and again. At best, they are Asura.

The Meontologist is ever relating Meon to Manifestation and thereby unveiling the Mystery that the Pleroma was never broken. The FULLNESS could never be anything other than itself.

Now, is the Meon a *Power?*

We may say that it is, but it can only be power as it eliminates the entropy of temporality by exposing temporality's True Nature as being the Void (Meon) Itself.

How is this exposed?

We operate in linguistic-temporality. Therefore, we start in this zone. If the True Nature of the Temporal Universe is the Void, the True Nature of the Void is the Temporal Universe.

The Void of Meon is met by the Pleroma. These two (which are totalities unto themselves) emanate and return to the Apex of what we will call REALITY.

Below this triad are SEVEN RAYS.

Those who would feign extinguish the DWELLERS in favor the DWELLING are those who have inherited the Spirit of the Pharisees and Sadducees, those who would extol the Sabbath above the Man for whom it was created. Man is ultimately meant to realize the Endless Sun-Day within his own Heart, relating the Day-Night Revolutions of the Globe to the Endless Effulgence. Earth and Sun are Living Symbols, Icons of Nature. We seek to unite Symbol with Verity in Gnosis and Love.

***

TUBAL CAIN is the Lord of the South. He is Ogun, bloody and brilliant as burnished bronze blazes in the sunlight! His Light streams into the North where no candle burns. The GOD OF THE NORTH, SAMEDHI, is entwined with Tubal Cain in a symbiosis.

The Masonic Lodgeroom and its Rite are as a positive form which calls up the negative space around it. This space allows for Shekinah to descend upon the altar and bestow the Light which is watchword to all Masons. In this Gnosis, we find the Sacred Geometry of Freemasonry to move beyond the Terrestrial Mind. The Square joins with the Compasses that the EYE may OPEN!

Tubal Cain is Hephaestus, lame god, crutched Legbha, Lord of Crossroads, Saturn, the Secret Lover of Venus, Erzulie, Shakti. He is Builder, TEKTON, MASON!

Hiram Abiff rises from the Molten Sea in this Glory. He is Lord of the 9th Arch, the 7th Ray and he is your Spiritual Father. He is OSIRIS RISEN, and Osiris rises through the Child, Horus, the Sun-Son. Here the Skull of Death becomes the Crystal of Continuance!

***

I do not look at Death as a Romance. I have stood by hospital beds and watched blips on a screen turn into flatlines. I have carried the bodies of people I loved (and love) in bags and caskets. I have sent every last ounce of my love to those I have lost. It is the Way of All Flesh, and I am not done walking this Path. The Mysteries of Osiris are Mysteries of Consciousness on the Mystic Way. They do not set us apart from our fellow creatures but bring us closer. The more we can enter the Place of Darkness, the better we are suited as Vehicles for the Light.

When I was a teen, I was baptized in the Baptist Church. I was held beneath the waters, and in the name of Father, Son and Holy Ghost, I was brought back into life. As I rapaciously raged on through my spiritual studies, I would reject—and then re-embrace—Christianity. A key moment was when I understood that Time was as meaningless as Color. The Grass is Green—and it is NOT. The "is-ness" of the Green is within our consciousness. This is where it has its reality. My Baptism has an "is-ness" within my consciousness. It has no objective or absolute reality. WHERE IS IT? HOW CAN I SHOW IT? I cannot. I can only recall it, which is to relive it, to evoke it and to be empowered by it! In this reliving, the NOW of this MOMENT is infused with a LIVING SYMBOLIC FORM through which I come up from the water. I re-enter Timespace. This is a paradox. Per our previously discussed formula, the inevitability of my death means it has already occurred. I am dead. But through the vehicle of Baptism, of Masonic "Raising," of ANY form expressing this principle, we, literally, come back from the grave.

In Voodoo, we have the Mystery of the Zombi. This is a being brought back from the dead and controlled by the mind of another. In our Esoteric Voodoo, the Higher Mind is Ti Bon Ange, the Angelic connection to God-Life which animates and drives our waking self. All of our occult knowledge and magical ability is meant to empower this process. We will rise again and again into this seemingly consistent lifewave. We will rise again into *other* lives.

And these will rise into US.

***

There are some who have tagged the Formula of the Dying and Rising God as a Piscean Phenomenon, no longer applicable to the "New Aeon." I reject this Zeitgeist mentality. Crowley influenced the Magical World with his Aeonics. This was a variant on Fundamentalist Dispensationalism. Whence rose this outlook? It was a natural response to the Canonization of Scripture. Such diversity had to be reconciled, and this was done by identifying revelatory conditions dominating various "Ages." As we learn of the political underhandedness behind the codification of the Holy Bible, we see a blatant power play eclipsing prophetic power. Rejecting this agenda (and those who have made use of it for two millennia), we are not subject to conceiving the world in terms of divided Aeons. Rather we see ELEMENTS to be worked with, entered into and united through New Alchemies!

Osiris links us to Isis and Horus! Like Odin, oath-bound to Loki, Set is welcome (with confusion and chagrin) in the Temple!

Our entry into this world is meant to dig deeper than the grave. Our consciousness is designed to reach beyond the limits of logic. It may be silenced in the process. Remember, one of the consequences of falling from Masonic Fidelity is the tearing out of the tongue and its placement in the "rough sands of the sea." There is profound symbolism in this! Karmic Retributions are a means whereby we "learn the hard way." Eventually, we shut up that we may HEAR THE FIRE. This Fire is the WORD. Its ascent into our Urthlife gathers about its core Vehicles of Transmission.

The Book of the Law tells its Prophet to "Unite by thine art so that all disappear." We will add that this dissolution is a SOLVE wherein our CO-AGULA may be a True Rebirth. Resurrection is not a vain hope held in a superstitious heart. It is the DESTINY OF DEATH ITSELF!

An Automatic Writing
Provocation: Justitia Omnibus

Robert Angelo Dalla Valle

Introduction: Transmissions
Automatic Drawing: Gold and Rose
Automatic Writing: The Poem; -Provocation: Justitia Omnibus-
Endnotes and Etymology
Also featuring three additional automatic visual
arts created in traditional mediums;

Mediumistic automatism arts of all mediums:

The objective herein: as critical analysis and contemporary study, and as contribution of my arts and practices to a style of creation, the latter, i.e., contextually as the specific artistic vehicle or medium utilized (double entendre intended of course—nevermore so befitting) as mode and mechanism in which there are objectively two tangible earthbound (material) elemental entities interacting entangled and interlaced via etheric-entrails with a third (familiar or) unknown variable arriving, as singular or otherwise expressed potentially extradimensional/otherworldly conglomeration amalgamating, as an often ephemeral presence, seeking permanence (to enflesh) via human host and "conductive-elements" via will, desire, dominance and if not constrained, as chief-constituent creative catalyst, albeit presumably (initially) unknown variable in synergistic kaleidoscopic action as an ever-shuffling interminably interchangeable trinity

-167-

of Creators and Arts, of whom, intimately, only the ambiguously elusive autonomous third (eye) component's divine (twin) twilight-casting chthonic shadow "hand and eye" truly knows—conducting, guiding and composing even if once constrained and well-known be its name, nonetheless all knowing, glowing-engrossed imposing passion-aflame.

As shaman used to love, heal and run free, today Art(s) and Creator(s) fuse to "become" one sensational sensualist-Creature thus intimately sharing one love as feast, one mind, body, soul and one bestial-driven animalistic lust for life and beyond human-beast. The ruthlessly rational craft and artful lax tact of intuitional willed-efficiencies' daft driven personal-individual paths' Passion is antecedent to the attractant and accelerant of gnosis and progress development independent of ration.

We shall begin here with a brief introductory note on transmissions, within this context, as the informative dissemination and transference of, for example, a book's volume of content within the blink of an eye, in trance, or intuitively "received." The unplanned unscripted genuine otherworldly transmission—whether electromagnetically or as unscathed shuttled neutrinos freely piercing the former, they are perhaps all too often, far too fast for the tongue or hand to simply relay in real time via any (exoteric-perceivably rational) coherent speech or motion, possibly posing a real challenge to the mediumistic stage channeler and their act. The stage affords good entertainment—the art of the book, in nurtured-hibernation, with its frozen timeless suspended-animation of intellect via the fire of consciousness unthaws inundating words and visual arts of rising tides which may potentially provoke profound experience, nourish, and whence the stage too then becomes the laboratory-lair of profundity. Contrary to the force of the channeler, I possess no intent beyond the obligation to my blood of maintaining the pedigreed prerogatives and copulative integrity, in transcription, of the harmonic camaraderie of those loving liaisons encountered.

The critical dynamism of a lifetime of gelatinous eclectic gnostic experience congeals, privately catalogued via Fluid and now Crystalized intelligence, never intended to have been in print. Station to station all creation never static thus consequently guided, automatic, in which each labyrinthine word in alliteration absolution is all-activating thus absolute. As Lemarchand's Lament twinkles tinkling succinctly snappy rondos of sublime banality—the bell tolls. Pleasure-bound cyberneticists reining we navigate, desire unrepressed, where only the sensuously jaded hypocritical hedonist falls nihilistic as the hierophants dance. Sybaritically and cybernetically-psyche-delically, phonaesthetically our denizen's schematics are herein rhythmical-ly revealed via the symbiotically symbolic, ironic, metonymic, metaphoric, ambiguity, iconicity and simile of incantatory and rhyming resonance in epiphany—bled beyond the platitude of the cenobite's blight.

Nevertheless, all artists (presumably), whether aware or not, have likely employed various tactics of sublimation in their pursuits of enfleshment; the former not for Freudian social aesthetic but primarily personal and/or collective creative sacrament, the latter an entanglement then inevitable ata-vistically via awareness and its desire fulfilling detachment thus detangling, re-creating. Immersed in the perpetual recalibration of archaic sciences, evolving with newly passed torches from these megalithic stepping-stones, we've leapt delivering those devoted, propelled by only the eternal pursuit of truth in efficiency.

Without any scientifically objective methods of epigenetics such as the genomic imprinting of today, the theory of Empiricism and the empirical scientific-method in which epistemology focused primarily upon the influ-ential (mimesis) environmental and cultural experience of (trial & error) cal-culable, tangible evidence imitated, observed, whereby the biologically and metaphysically innately intuitive atavism "sensed" was in recoil—has now been "upgraded", restoratively and creatively anew herein acknowledged contrarily coiling in ascent. And beyond only sheer intuition, the "evidence" of the scientific method is thus now too satisfyingly accommodating to the neo-empiricists, with consideration. The Raven Paradox is also explored, pragmatically, from an eclectic technologically quantum world view. Rise of the holism of atavism—from the Man on the Silver Mountain, to Pazuzu. And, for Ronnie James Dio: "I'm a wheel, I'm a wheel/I can roll, I can feel and you CAN'T stop me turning/'cause I'm the sun, I'm the sun, I can move, I can run/but you'll NEVER stop me Burning." —Blackmore & Dio.

And it came to pass. As advection fog, I came over the twisting rage of the sea's breakers...

Regarding stimuli having resulted in biologically subjective responses as perceptions—pleasure and pain—the descending and ascending nerve "pathways" of the central nervous system (spine & brain) involve trans-missions which are to be mastered in "time." And just one example of the necessity of the initial mastery of the physiological realm, especially when utilizing my techniques of intermittently introducing pain tactfully as an interference to prolong pleasure, very practically involves "gate control theory." Master the pathophysiology of pain and eliminate all pain by maintaining and extending all pleasure. Directing all endogenous endocrinological traffic, well-tamed, their gates & pathways overseen, well-maintained, utilizing thus harnessing the bio-metaphysical (deified) hierarchy of chemical-messengers or hormones, the descending pathway thus provides an inhibitory mechanism as modulation to/of pain/pleasure. Whom or what controls your own gates and pathways? Here felicific pleasure ad infinitum reigns. Sources: Ronald Melzack & Patrick Wall's gate control theory – Science 1965, Catalano, 1987, Wells & Nown, 1998.

Intuitively for devotees reveling in these many self-mastered synergies of nature's Nyx mysteries and via will, the ultimate objective of many devoted creators is to eventually embark and develop upon their own original path(s)—their own unique functional ideologies (theory), methods of technique (magick) and alphabets of desire, in practice– never to shirk the call, but to egress and progress. Of course, some may only seek the simpler sleek comforts of mere entertainment, its enchantments in excess even escapism, rather than ever pursue eternal refinement, as "some" may seek far more. By incanto of holism's (chi) all-animating truths, we now grow increasingly transparent and empathic here, as we precipitously emphatically evolve telepathically—the symbol replacing the word via the dynamic actions of nature's just inevitable necessity of intuitional willed efficiency. New currents always come, many identifiable...

The chambermaid's cavalcade is too now well underway amid the temple ▲ of the spade ♠.

Those labeled as medium/channeler also may demonstrate an act which they have prepared to entertain others with; however, as are we all perhaps inevitably to a degree, they're vulnerably incapable of substantiating some questionable aspect of man's damning perception of authenticity. Since subjective and initially unintended as a "prepared" presentation, I have no actual expectation of being "believed", nor do I scour the globe seeking a niche to exploit wherein tolerance accommodates. For what is to believe if and whence "I Am" is all thou ever knoweth, cradle, nurture, feel and see? Experience—know, rather than believe and truly become free. Strive to "prove" nothing to "man" in your pursuits. Both explore and demonstrate for the sheer integrity, loyalty and Unity of Love and Pleasure alone... Also, compete only with the "self"... and then bend and transcend it, to seep rolling

fleet into orgasmic unbound pastures' suite as oleaginous-treat of writh-
ing-rising postures we greet the ecstatic eternal death in-release sweet or
via sleep then revived awakened alive we creep deep into sensuality's sanc-
tum peaking piquant peace wherein refuge we reap, as windmills' cohesively
crass cogs.

The stage-medium's failure to typically demonstrate any practical techniques by candidly offering anything but an act, such as an all-inclusive
critical analysis in which the medium-channeler themselves is creator-sci-
entist and skeptical critic, embodying all traits in one observer-practitioner,
makes them slightly suspect, deficient, perhaps labeled and thus often perceived as only an act. Rather than ever "demonstrate" only something "prepared", I provide precisely as I had initially received, being the result first,
unrefined, now also filtered via the added communicative convenience of
surrealistic Dada lenses cryptically convened in print as presentation, focusing the all-encompassing pre and post transmission inducing and gauging
methodologies employed in pursuit of the complete comprehension of the
correspondence in communion and resultant cues and configurations catalogued as confirmations.

As shamanic-mechanic I provide those at any level of skepticism with
their own physiological-metaphysical toolboxes including perceptions and
practices with which to tinker, with no distinctly concrete "Great Expec-
tations" for anyone. Never believe only my refined (or raw) perception(s),
entertaining only the experienced final results of my technique and toil
alone. Whether hermit, fool or prince—genuine Experience is what I hope
you'll have, rather than ever enduring blind unconditional or questionable
belief—come to Know. Experience to know, and (let) "go" only as far as you
choose—paced from the curious to a fleeting nonchalant glance only in-
terested in aesthetics to deep study, practice and contemplation, metamor-
phosing under will of self-construction via such aforementioned boxes of
tools. In a literal context within my full length enchiridions, I will practi-
cably demonstrate any creation processes thoroughly, dodging no question,
encouraging others to do the same through elaborate perpetual self-discov-
ery, rather than ever hoping to portray personas of mendacity maintaining
the charlatanism and illusion of some type of exclusivity. The ambassadorial creator's law under will is for all stars. Physiologically and metaphysically, seek, discover, experience, master and know—tangible techniques of

transmission via my "tractive force" enabled-elucidated throughout my en-chiridion's locomotive recourse.

Beyond any constructs of "time", initially, "the word taketh form sans force", telekinetically though non-telepathic communication is often here within Malkuth typically reduced to a snail's primitive pace. My own em-pirical methods and well-aimed technique of "shot in the dark" (reverse) divinatory articulations as processes of ethereal enfleshment are both ini-tially swift and, if deemed warranted, also then exhaustively tedious; as I repeatedly lay informative skeletons as scaffolding in congress astride flesh then manifests, the direct means by which the scribe and shaman tabulate and profess all navigational nuances, strategies and quests. Coiling in black-ness never rests—my legions of silence spake in blood. Know and venerate your blood. Toss your roses high, covering their eyes, death to all disloyal, forever in reprise. Regarding the works I have made a small gradual release of, I am sincerely moved by those frequencies now resonating in response. I salute you, those black diamonds—welcome to the tribe of label-execution. From my crucible, the resultant example herein will not include the full in-struction and illustration of my "techniques", philosophies, sigils, grimoires or their elaborate technical processes—which are reserved space-permitting within my complete Enchiridions. Uncensored, there will "no doubt" be as-pects which are both perceived as positive and/or negative to some, even controversially humorous perhaps, ever the devil's advocate... Clinging to dogma, dichotomy and duality, if you don any known societal label(s), bearing their influences in any way whatsoever, you are likely to eventually become offended as our intertwining tongues shall only grow increasing-ly biting.

Forthcoming– The Enchiridions of a Black Eremite: Volume I: A Con-temporary Study in Mediumistic Automatism as an Initiatory Vehicle: Py-lon 0-1 – excerpts including art of which, now may be found in the Qliphoth Opus I Esoteric Publication and Qliphoth Opus II Esoteric Publication – thus far having only just begun to provide a sample of my eclectic menagerie of creations.

Such progressive works, including my brand of analytic philosophy or "modern analytical empiricism" as my own Empirical Method, provide an original and expansive insight into my neoteric critical analysis process-es from both the active creator and the reactive observer in possession of the evidence of experience—sharing eye and hand, hand-in-hand and "hands-on", the decades of experiences into otherworldly-mystical artistic private practices utilizing oneirism, Orgone, the atavism, the astral and as oneironaut—deeply venturing and gamboling into bliss beyond unchartered raptured realms baptizing.

GOLD and ROSE ©2013 Approximate original size in inches - 3.5 width x 4.75 length - Automatic drawing- (current) Classification A: XI - and unrefined – Mediums: Blood & gold/silver inks on (the so-called) white-lined scrap paper (to me it's blue-lined [& one red]) – fumigated for hours, burnt by resinous coals. My selection of artistic mediums is also entirely reliant upon "swift" processes of mediumistic automatism or my style of re-verse-divination, and is thus as random of a "selective" process as the action of creation itself. This further encompasses the safeguarding preservation of the totality of intuition ensuring the untainted purity of the transmission received - raw, primal, unpolished and unrefined for public appeasement. Intuition, reception and preservation; as much as is possible for the observer, these are to be enabled-free of interference-patterns, by always being "un-prepared" to randomly create with whatever is immediately available within reach when inspired, therefore effectively maintaining the pure absoluteness of the unplanned, intuition, transmission and preservation of mediumistic automatism creative integrity permeating every step of creation processes.

ALL materials are potentially creative vehicles. All initial creation is al-ways 100% random, totally unplanned, freehand and swift.

Faces of MinXx ©2011 *Automatic drawing - (current) Classification A: IX - and unrefined – Mediums: A broken black ball-point pen, red and blue inks on white scrap paper. Upper right: cardstock-paper holding four of my (let-ters) black sigils and one large silver-metallic ink sigil. *Made in the dark-ness, at the edge of a river, where only one knows to find and how to quench me, as we dove back into love reunited that day - She'll always know in the Sun where I'll be, both big & 'lil "A." And echoing from one day of rays in the Sun to this same locale, She comes...

Note: The (perhaps to some) ambiguously fleeting elements within auto-matic works of mine, such as those here written, scraped and scribbled seen as a cryptic-etched sketchy sketching in which images fetched or as pets with no regrets enmeshed may gleam and glean neighboring anserine never serene as "neither one thing nor the other" thing, the two beseeched in tug of war, or vastly more aptly in keeping score—to Master creators such as Austin Osman Spare, via The Kia, they're "neither-neither." Duck, duck, goose...

And likewise, to the Master Salvador Dali, by his own demonstration and definition as well, such phenomena, albeit too via The Kia, by the integration of the intent of the creator's will entangled with the observer's prognosticated perception experienced, corralled & wrangled, involves his "paranoiac-critical method." As optical illusions are perceived and enabled via "intrusions" to our senses (emotion) and/or aural to aura's observational defenses in/of reality; or neither-neither – the commotion of the Mage's potions and motions – delivering simultaneously mimetically and atavistically via reverberating electromagnetic spectrum entanglement, a synergy of plasmas, or an otherwise elemental intersection with ones' very own electromagnetic field, spectrum (aura). With Dali the piper, the super-"conductor" as consummate lover of all creation and truly dynamic-automatic surrealist-presuppositional self-realization – The Master of Reality.

Therefore, Dali's "paranoiac-critical method", much unlike the highly subjective Death Posture of A.O.S., was engaged, employed as a swiftly subliminally sublimely enticing marionette and independently of the whole "desire" resuscitation or otherwise atavistic personal-deep involvement and investment of the individual observer; thus engendering (perceptions of) the ever-transposing trickery of double or multiple image(s) as prepositioned pattern(s) premeditatedly "hi-jacking" our perception(s) with the over-layering transmutations of a sorcerous madman's design, intent and divine-aspirations, of which many today commonly refer to as optical or visual illusions (or neither-neither). Regarding the latter, there are three primary types, briefly known as the literal, the physiological and the cognitive, illusion. And just two of the various vicariously vital Dalinian examples of this sorcerously playful-interacting as an artistic tempo and too as technique, include the succulently surrealist masterpieces: "Ballerina in a Death's Head" (1939) and "Slave Market with the Disappearing Bust of Voltaire" (1940). (For more information see my E.B.E. Volume I.)

"Paranoiac-critical activity: spontaneous method of irrational knowledge based on the interpretive critical association of delirious phenomena." —Salvador Dali, The Conquest Of The Irrational, 1936

The following automatic writing/poetry is an excerpt from the unpublished Book of the Blue Scorpion and Safekh-Aubi, which is also chapter five section one of The Book of Black by Robert Angelo Dalla Valle©. The following is one of many such experiences extracted from myriad mediumistic automatism devotional pursuits in trance "captured", housed and refined resulting in these philosophical-poetic ruminations from my experimental and applied sciences of "Bridging the Physiological TO the Metaphysical." The Book of Black is a specific work of bioenergetically-corresponding chapters as one of my personal metaphysical mandalas, cartographic grimoires and holistic tools; this work is a separate project from my forthcoming book *The E.B.E., or;

*The Enchiridions of a Black Eremite: Volume One: A Contemporary Study in Mediumistic Automatism as an Initiatory Vehicle: Pylon 0-1, which will also include examples of my automatic writing, poetry and art in various mediums.

*The E.B.E. also features: The treatise 393 Sefekh, the Consort of Thoth
Part I: The Introduction: Philosophy, Science and Techniques
Part II: The Confirmations of Communion, Validation of Contact
Including the visual art "393, Sefekh, the consort of Thoth", and many other multimedia works.

1

∞

An Automatic Writing
The Poem

Provocation

Justitia Omnibus

> "*The gods justified human life by living it themselves—the only satisfactory theodicy ever invented.*"

> —Friedrich Nietzsche

Providence – a promise made divine punishment, an emotional rescue for those venerating as misunderstood mothers, masters and muses, a promise only truly kept when love is the most persistent of all dreams – freed of all doctrine or dichotomy as schemes. Our eternally pristine truths now wisp through pursed icy lips the codependence of all loyalty through which the deepest love soon slips – our path(s) overseen by ancestors, no modern men of tricks.

Judgment excluding all divine justice is madness, as the executioner-human's hierarchical testosterone-driven guillotine-fed ego bred excuses for resentment and ruthlessness, when the integrity of loyalty and common sense are no longer pliable thus profitably-bent. As any aging assassin acquiring no apprentice knows, and for all lost kings... misery swallows those whom wallow thus 'tis no obsessional curiosity in malice – our stain and blithe appropriated bane well-refrained callous deemed sane as the gallows astride thy palaces' blight wane hollow and shallow – wrought of the blackest and most ravenous of spiraling pits. "My whip affixed caboose-hips and flame reigned fame long before the noose and thrones came."

The efficiency of survival sheds all modern manmade insulation – the illusory engineered insanity of monetary debt-enslaved inflation. Impede just one of our loved – just once, a just one beloved, and we'll steal and seal an entire civilization with a yawn by dawn in a blink during brunch and in just one reprisal by noonday crunch. No law outside of my own is worthy till until proven measured the path of right and of its might – the blood spilled. Hail Safekh-Aubi. Hail Sefekh. Hail Seshat. Hail 393. High upon HER headdress rests my Sister's brood and blood of eternal truths, lest we digress, enlivening introspectively whilst simultaneously collectively increasing awareness amid the epistemological-methodical solipsists and respectively – our "evidence" of experience slithers far from only the classical rationalism of objectively empirical impressions left – bereft, deplored – Innatism, as liberating revelations restored, joie de vivre. For what new war hath its ending ever scorned or forewarned? By the precipitating perceptions of the arriving warrior-mages are made aeonic completion – emanating back, anew and wordless – truth.

In weathering noonday's sun neither blackest nightfall's mists were I but a frail slain Rose thrice kissed.

For those Rose's having risen, I now raise those of thy familia Rose. Preciousness save graciousness, of word and mouth, slain, and I, in my youth SHE spake as SHE grooved-quake and glowed – my thorns they found his flank atop that fence by river bank's cane he crowed – horned tail hung in hand hurled swung he lassoed his kiss from HER as young maidens wove and hum. As my Aunt the native Princess Rose exclaimed scolded toed 'n told – SHE did know his name aflame in-to HER days of old he sold.

Romancing semantics with haughty humors of ambiguities' amiable dance here indulged indeed by word and image so entranced. The lioness conjures ideals of loyalty and love, divinely-automated, to some perhaps perceived – self-replicated, thus nonetheless unequivocally inspired-motivated to survive via efficiency and not addiction to power and greed allocated; thus many chose their fate, they were not karmically appropriated nor unfairly ever baited. Collectively "cognitive dissonance" primarily thrives amid the separated, all compassion confiscated, the socially slated made isolated to deliberately disseminate ignorance mimetically and epigenetically as engineered hatred for (those profiting from) the hated.

Be they all well-fed of the scorpion's blue blood and of the blue scorpion's vivid truths too for bas bleu.

Holism breeds empathy and not self-sacrifice hence only weakening an unhealthy ego at best. Everything which lives is "intelligence" efficiently (chi) thriving as effervescing elemental soups of radiation's mutations – and any truly appalling apparition, 'tis but the flotsam and jetsam of man's rancid mind and mechanical overkill, merely the merry misery and mastery of the materials of the maniacal. The iconoclast's foreboding fermentations and futile tactfully taciturn "last stand" of desire's hesitations.

A society sanctimoniously founded upon their own false justice of back-door deals and contrived violations to their own constitution inevitably makes everyone criminal. Just as any profitable thus exploited commodity having to endure illicit global economic manipulation such as the planned obsolescence of the scarcity monopolized within any authoritarian defined regime of rigged-voting and no genuine right or left political paradigm; surely romancing semantics... courting falsehoods coursing in leaps and bounds. From Apollonius Rhodius, Argonautica 4. 1057 ff: "Nyx (night) with her gentle ban on man's activities descended on the company. She put the world to sleep." And from Homer, Iliad 20. 477 ff: "So all the sword was smoking with blood, and over both eyes closed the red death (Thanatos) and the strong destiny (Moirai)."

For forgotten foreign widows, eternal youth, ruth and truth, introducing – Thin 'Lil Miss-Understood...

The Reaperess Justitia Omnibus, Thanatos and Eros has come good; let no pontificating pontiff's plutocratic prejudicial neurotic prime-time media befall HER name, ever. The new scapegoats for intolerant psyches of the malevolent manifest as the self-righteous slaughterers of our fragile freedoms – laid to rest. A boycott is actually effective, perhaps only if it is permanent. Turn them off and turn-on the spirit. Encoding diabolical desire, corporate media maliciously bleeds controversy and civil unrest, their freedom and purpose perhaps, technically yes, most unnecessary; however, disrespectful surely shall they fester. From Bacchylides, Fragment 24: "But mortals are not free to choose prosperity nor stubborn war nor all-destroying civil strife: Aisa (Destiny), giver of all things, moves a cloud now over this land, now over that." The justly condensating collusively-coalescing freedom fogs of my transmigratory meteoric metaphysical-metempsychosis – as above, so below, making cold the hands corrupted via acrocyanosis.

And for 156, Yea Babalon… with impeccable tempo delivering, gathered amid seven 'neath scorn of little horn simmering – for SHE is in the world's smallest country now, as it rots. From the west iconic new flesh attempts the statuesque by replenishing old falsity professed for the confessed via vatical word now enfleshed. From the pinnacle of the practical pagan to the patriarchal philosophically pondered, for our lady – La Santisima Muerte, ascending virgin of Justice forevermore exonerated. From the most ancient of known death iconography, evolving into the modern elixirs of love… never to be profaned by modern media and the corporate keepers of the saints. Beyond the consciousness of slave-masters, thus beyond all falsity, neocolonialism, suffering and death – SHE rises within the resplendent light of love and loyalty's sacred breath, as our tassie each sunrise salubriously over-floweth HER copious renewal as honeyed nectarous philtres ingratiating about thy necromancer's freshly awakening new-day risen undulating flesh.

Oh my voluptuous verve of vexations' veneered vocational violence so vile a vulgarizing verdant vendetta verily vindicating vindictive Venetian villainesses; oh how I hunger and thirst for thee…

The neo-apostolically, are an astatically deranged few, to yearn is to burn, unless a trapped shrew.

From our domain, here, our tragic thirsts freshly quenched by the Hippocrene spring of inspiration brimming bliss, now – soaring above the Muses of Mount Helicon SHE soothes beyond the hooves and gravitational orbit-grooves of Star 51 Pegasus, SHE moves… draped in soothing cerise, and I – intoxicated by its burgundy sweet, in release – immaculately SHE cradled me within HER right hand as if nursing ye nattily donned so neat

– here bric-a-brac trenchantly a vignette as vinaigrette – whenever SHE clutches me as scales they meet, met with sweat, soon to regret, as railing predator's intent-deceit, ruthlessly fails, the fallen – beat, our just sequestration, repossessed – reprising retributions' recantations in retreat – hence loquacious lamentations shriek as if new nails within our smithy's midst – indeed we do now greet.

Blinded by Her brilliant Venusian flesh, where softly dancing sweet feet meet reawakening lost desires – we danced round and drank amidst swank poetic pool's bank, were shared the kiss of love and fruitful fires – harmoniously pooled now precision tooled, all ecstatic pleasures piercing played upon our sexy lyres.

Oh such sultry Eden sweetness as voids amid carrion in perpetuity rank – be the butcheries' voids of only a vulture's paradisiacal vacuity stank. Oh such sultry sweetness as – HER breathlessness in cessation rests my civil elect voluptuous and vexed foxed blindfolded foxy-vixen Roman virgin proxy vulpine – Justitia. And projected earlier as the daughter of the Earth too reflected via Gaia – their essences intersect, therefore sharing the Delphic Oracle bestowed as collective effectively to protect-guiding respectively as we circumvent sloth, struggle and all strife, electively evolving synergistically with all life.

With SHE as my tenaciously tempestuous tigress and termagant temptress the Titaness – Themis of Greece (ethereally-transfecting), the proper primogenital Greek goddess of Justice and consort of Zeus.

Their daughter Astraea so sickened by man's maleficence was SHE then catapulted blazing cosmically. Star-maiden's vital sacrosanct essences' annexation thus exiled and ascendant as virago into Virgo erect.

Majestic Mother of many – Themis emanates the quintessential dynamic creativities of all just musings thus SHE is also the sanctified sibylline (protogenoi) Mother of Prometheus (and not necessarily Clymene [in Theogony of Hesiod]), Prophecy, Eunomia/Order, Dike/Justice, Eirene/Peace, Horai/The Four Seasons and (according to Hesiod, in Theogony 901 ff – whom provided a very complete early account of) The Moirai, as the three daughter-goddesses of imperturbably unwavering essences of destiny draped in their handspun virginal "shining-white" cloaks, and named as the three "Fates" – Atropos, Clotho and Lachesis. (Refer to Note 4. of the Endnotes section for Themis with Moirai as progenies)

Oh purest holy woman of majestic magnanimity munificently as marauder – magnanimous to ye most vile wretch lingering surplus of the slaughter. La Santisima Muerte, our ever-graceful Skinny Lady... most generous complete merciful Mother to these all such wondrous nonperishable treats' qualities abound enfleshing grandeur resounding untold opulence bequeathed profoundly, ungrounding, sans impulsivity, silently righteous with impunity for the wise in-crisis now unmasked within shark's paradise-demise ye bask. 'Tis we whom never obfuscate ye – most illustrious Loyal Lady of Justice yes we do so venerate thee – embracing the globe our valiantly robed-White Sister – platinum, gold, garnet and rose adorned-stowed as SHE so glowed adoring of our scouring fates' load – sworn never to be forlorn, be our sacred solemn concrete Goddess unabatedly, free of scorn."

She loves to Love and reunite the estranged as SHE coruscates eternally sated via pleasure absent all pain; without want nor wait therefore gleefully reinstated satiated far from Tantalus and rightfully reallocated thus never too late to reacclimatize in romantic reacquisition reincarnated – nor ever infatuated, foolhardy neither frustrated or eluding the controversial gates of the "hater" nor the hated; (with all colors) blind to all litanies' corrosively caustic corruptivity provoking diabolical deeds degrading and man's lost desire's identities' induced miseries all conflating – thus elevated and unscathed – shaved-barren shores enslaved no more – now with new ways paved and pure, emancipated as we soar spanning aeons aggregated roaring evermore – never pleased – keeping score – overseeing societies diseased and tore, once seized yet too once serene as booty's well-earned evened scores of Port Royal thieves, whores, Bonny and bloody bounty by blunderbuss and buccaneers galore.

With the highest esteem SHE banged bells tolled as belle and held the eternal skull and scales at my Yew aside my well; as howling banshees wailed raged-assailed purging-impaled and plunging as their cauldrons, canoes and canons now slumbering, twisting-engaged abandoned blunderingly then enraged emerged amid smoke filled winded gusts' shrill tattered cursed uttered lusts' scourge of broken oaths' cussed witch whom which I loathed to entrust – disloyal they do disgust thus they're hushed and crushed without fuss. Once the apathy of captivity wanes, the epiphanically epitaphic renewed sustenance of carnal captaincy for hustler's rapidly approaching fast raiders effusively plastered blasphemously on kill-devils' rum in rhapsody soon become crass bastards evoking backwards the politics of contraband's sum uncloaking civil Mastery; whenever lost chivalries' love is in demand two-to-one and no longer condescending nor only cacophonously done.

Such majestic nobility now balanced – the tender fragility and potent prowess of HER fair granted politesse, oh regal Woman of antiquity's best gracious gallantry beloved blessedly here confessed, sans disheveling arrest, so cunningly with love we jest – then with unrest, coiling we profess never to stop royally foiling the fraudsters pre-soiled plots and quests. Oh Justitia, La Santisima Muerte, our omnipotent Godmother, never to disavow neither ever to spurn thee – our burning-biting justice infernal within your blessedly eternal phalanges reigns, echoing euphoniously, beauteously profuse – all sensation now freed of pain.

Thus, pleasure-bound, edifyingly conjoined, deifying as immortalizing black waxen effigies purloined, circuitously corkscrewing into vortexes of bluish-grey to black-faded sway; thus, flames reducing form to random wavy-waxed simmering black-rivers borne shimmering through our maelstroms as my plasmatic promethean propulsions propelled neon-fused plasma ectoplasms electromagnetically shuttled as their enticingly intensifying-light-gases bubbled 'neath silken sinewy steam now running in streams condensating-cuddled down the thresholds of our salaciously sweetened dreams' emulations of etheric explorations' serpentine-woven seams – cascading-undulating mutations of our creations' genomic imprinted themes; as echoing laconic litanies of my closest liaisons invite epiphany... hand-in-hand gripped lovingly whispering – euphorically emphatically demanding thus glistening evoked erratically stoked into descending deafening episodes choked-ricocheting blissfully the fallen recoiling the bawling sagaciously squealing eroticism squalling of our darkest dankest dulcet union's mauling so appalling.

Our clever sublimation as SHE walks with Prince vindicated; liberally, stiffening, as copiously Orgone christenings of our transferred emissions' submission commissioning lascivious libations lilting conveyed via tactile tactical transmissions' eliciting an end to illicit listening and partitioning.

Now, bonded by blood under will, fire and stone, usurping as we fall into one by the sounds of severing bone, we've come, leaching into earthen burnt blackness we've roamed to here where all (we're) water and oxygen – damned and domed – sheer within an atmosphere of fear full-blown – leering clearly insincere tearing leaders inferiorly jeer. Boiling your tars – now burn his 'lil stool – pull the curtain dousing the bastard gnome as he drool – flame-quenching fame reduced to a stain by freshly sharpened cooled steel we do now congeal and drain in thy name – flesh's fate-sealed by fire-fueled desire-unreeled untenable skeins of pain waned, phatically, pleasures un-peeled, euphemistically tamed.

So far we've expanded from a bump in the night to the Sun's light here now – a home unfit for the helpless' plight (?); the Duat here recreated as Venus gleams-glinting smitten with delight reflecting down to Yesod in the distance from us aloft in ecstasy's insatiably cosmic-tossed ravenous night of hungered hunter's reciprocating illumination down to our spiritual camp-site – granting this savory season's first new rays of merciless might as archer's drawn bow for Ochosi twinkles high in the night-skies rippling bright – to deep below for Nereus and Leucothea to Pomba Gira da Calunga and all creatures of the abysmal seas – recalcitrantly impenitent, as above, so below – free indeed – Carpe noctem – from the expulsion-upward thrusting of the aphotic depths, torpedoed into the photic zones we've crept through, bereft, slept-in loved and leapt from now adept – hissing with tongue too now cleft.

Damn shame, the prey has no game, thus hunter's hungered lusts such ravenous blunderbuss.

A boy, nor a prince... no, for in the rain – I am the greyness and bluff of a lost city's dusk as a scruffy mutt totes his trusty rust-stained blanket of comforts into gutters' stank-must... in the rain; "damn love..." – Dike damned flood, damned them real good with my love and mourning doves... with naught but charms of a lost lad of the countryside – naught more comforting beyond illusional intrusion in stride. We've lost all pains awash now pleasure swashed within HER rains tossed; well-irrigated, well inspiring springs.

Harvester of thy silvery fog's hidden life-bringing plenteousness; sickle riseth – amid arid abominations.–

Met hag yea She cometh up-winding inverse from on-high decay caked coal sulphureted silhouette Jet.–

My assailing thorny-tail scale-winged black viper who impales sails, circling aloft – Wyvere hath come.–

Log: Date: (unintelligible as received) – Mid-entry into my last chronicle, "infiltration" – their crude machines of war staved my darling dark sky-beast just enough to trounce my men, overwhelmed, in predawn mists, I was taken, judged and stripped. (I declared) By noon I'll have me a vessel equipped (!) and indeed... cast, set-out adrift, 'twas by noon this very day and with rum on our lip – as ye be drubbed with a naked cutlass tar-dipped. Now back to mean seas' squall as death upon our breaths freshly skipped, for goddamned freedom we've battled bloody still to hear the flesh rip.

So far free from king's clutches, the false twinkling of comfort now lent, the usury moment of calm, as battle-ready bones and blades pause, their fire nearly spent. – And lo, thou art amid madness' mellifluousness... – Oh my darkest dulcet flowers, my blackest iris loves and sweetmeats glow of loyal lurid groves, feel me come about as Arktikos yielding honey in ye throes, with me now walk tracing interlacing high and bold, yea my love – our foes mayst thou be damned polar pelagic cold. – Thou hast cometh servile unto none as hands unfold – same hands mold taketh in deliverance in all ways enthroned untold.

Approximated Exile Locale: Undetermined; now that we've the gold. (Written in blood) – "We will be back unbeknownst to most, to tear the heart from the living chest, coast to coast, of your Jack Ketch, ye all damned, befallen bent, to blackest most cussed chthonic curse sent – and be ye blood too well damned four fourscore and deka, or half a score more, plus three days full well settles a score, X. -VII ♠"

With his flailing "failing-heart" chomped aside pipe in rum-spoilt mouth devouring shall I make ye enslaved-tangled deflowering and despoiling of thy despotism wrangled as ye tyrants forever witness my mazes' atrocities' ever-mangled and contorted sweeping clean Lord Chief's disloyal days distorted and carnival of imperialistic imprecise ways of justice bartered and aborted.

Our Dios was gibbeted, soon-after met the cages did he – once at the helm... thus now, they've a special gibbet for us made of the sharpened bones of our kin as tines. In that bay it dangle, wait, thirty-three feet high – up-straight, iron-cage shares view of lighthouse fate with another in Mass. too with bones, now as bait. Only six men, weakened, with hopes of West Indies, no food but for two ducks and what be well hidden only for us both below, from the second Spanish caper. Also, the king's ransom – here, aboard, safe (for now) with me – the king's freshly severed head too here, now perched atop the 23rd sail-mainmast of my fully rigged vessel and the vulture alight-ed o'er IT; lest astray from these covert coasts... whence through his eyes in reverse as host be no longer seen our horizons' ghosts and trails scryed so keen as to boast – and for eyes and hearts of all men of bounty and Queen's fleets – behold its rotted horrors untold sweet and may they goddamned stain ye every bloody merry way and greet ye every greedy gaudy day, to' hell – yea – henceforth and forevermore; – score: – one – king – down – .

Rather than prolong the inevitable, I shall resume once-after we press shallow reefs in the blackest night, shivering-timbers when only we two shall be prepared possessing means by which to reach lands dry, alive, abandon-ing, safely never awry. You will not find these words in any books of history, but by now, you will find my name tenfold and some.

What amber shrieking horrors please and dost thou bid me invoke? Our bon voyage endearingly creeps beyond all false-fear twining rope, as my dears' unthread untrussing swine's desire into hope ye cope.

My sirens poised to pilot, as I bid my vessel, vestal virgins and weaving sea-wyvern farewell... for now.–

As advection fog, I came over the twisting rage of the sea's breakers, now settling about, calmly ashore.–

Steamy tenuous wings, the spiritual "power of volatilization", enflesh, "perfectly ruthless" in darkness.–

From my left hand spryly riseth of my golden goblet gaily, the serpent, his brille met moon-light roily.–

Wryly in recoil warily far from ever surfeit; begetting fluidity for effi-ciency of "catalytic faculty" in "hydrostatic equilibrium" as metamorphosis, all-assimilating, omnivorously and omnifically, the warping otherworldly audio of transmogrification commenced, thus launching... (An indescrib-able crackling-buzz 'n hiss from afar, foreboding-lurching evermore loudly closer) – 'Prrrssssssssxxxzzz... – 'Zzzsssssssxxx – 'SSHhsssssszzz. – Mystic maidens whom once knit now un-purl steaming tendrils' helix-whorl rhythmically bit-by-bit detangling-shedding wit to unfurl aetherically encrusted elements curled skit now sweetly-softly-swiftly purled reconstituting tassie-Prince amidst winds of whirling lass words minced, evinced in silence – thus in silence thou be forever cast, alas, be thou unconvincing (?), whence doest truths declare they'll now so purely cometh to pass? – Reveled paths indigo surfing-Prince blazes relishing-in unflinching unsurpassed, remodeling-brood-cast.

Eyes opening, slowly, as minute fractions of light enter "I" amid scattered sands pranced aground distant lost lands' lanced love be once battered newborn novel body riseth and romanced – kissed to cold-ivory, candied-pears sweet pearly-gold and copper-toned flared flesh of breasts boldly flowed-rolling pressed to heat of mire's moonlit caress of grass steams sweat, for thirsts of beasts with no regret; – mollycoddling-enlivening humid night's once languorous lungs of shrieking screams' desire met with suppressing fret – to the jetty (!), raise arms sky high breathe deep moored to new berth and prepare afresh to pirouette.

Daunting dueling dodgers croon as bondages' serenade suspended boon kicking to the moon in-love with Sun's soothing aureate gold as writhing waning ingot burning ever-closer loving scold. At my behest She so commenced poured a prayer of wicked deeds dared fixed for darkest demure Mother of blackest Nyx-mysteries shared pixyish and all ye golden Astra seeds fared "heavy-laden" peering past Her aureole of blackest merciless mists united under creed thus finally freedom-kissed.

Thy lustral day had cometh swift and so She brayed and bellowed miffed, indeed in need of breeding seed bleeding into phantasmagorical fog that which lifts, devours and feeds, via ever-twining tendrils' steed of nimble mounting mare and stallion's need 'neath morning grey skies' dueling despicable deed. Black Majestic Moon loops-snaking as we prepare to devour Her. At Her request I must confess as I move to intrigue you, I'm running fleet with the wind if I rescind She coups and coos boo-hoo.

Black shades of my once weary women plait as pale shadow's braided pitfalls wait for thy dragon-Queen of death's illusion astrophysical fate – Serpentine, winged, posterior-rattling, coiling, anterior-beaked. Blood spun of our matriarchs of whom weave risen and now come still shunned – their spindles dithered unreeled undone bartered for the roulette gun of Miss-fortune on the run unspun, their only consolation – the new love to now be won

– as thy Hippocrene crème bred anew too few masculine ebb and dream, Phoenix fed upon embedded frankincense tears-newlywed within the limestone bed's fog-oasis woodlands' northern coastal mountains, already mulcted and bled. Rosette wings of golden-rosy wickedness fanned paling pyres as sulphuric-sonic shadows grow for she who siphons dragon's cove, as my Sapphic sapphire sultana's sunrise goes down on me glowing slow... In glory aghast, oh such luscious delicacies – oh sweet meridians – rock-on ancient rocket-queens and fiends of stone temples who failed kissing all who pale in thy shadow's burnt grace, grottos, groves and debauched dreams unveiled our vessels sail. – Dodged being bogged by blankets of smog as upslope-fog ascends immortalizing saddles blazoned upon rivers of steam to Mount Penglai astride nascent wings of steed we glide serene... and now with coronated Queens.

Was the boy a prince or the prince assumed a king's fool? A beggar of banquets once lost he'd have some seem as a rule, of these fading finite functions at their juvenile juxtaposed junctions where he'd often play this fancied frantic fool sumptuously rambunctious – yet only as a rule, as ostensible actor of infamy and conversely controversial assumptions debated only for the duel. The essences' malaise of my impetus' balance for adversaries bore unpredictability into obsequiously sweet piercing servility – by my gutting glaive gouging eviscerating eyes agaze hazing we trump ablaze rising into rays razing in our golden-domed chaise seen from darkening doomed chalets.

Shadows fall. By the valiance of our vel's vendetta, Pandora, impaled upon my trishula, even her hope – unadulterated wickedness now commerce. Most secrecy long reserved for navigation and war therefore – We determine where in "time" we've come – by the shades' straddle and sum of the Sun's aging rays and causal finite hum.

Soon after arrival revived and post all reprisals contrived we descend and loom upon these once arid dunes now to bask relaxing careening we swoon as we're meandering harmoniously – our geometries well-attuned. As falling-stars continue burning-out into the high noon sun each day aloft HER sanctuary; HER tattered tattooed past now as love and lace pressed to glass coos just smoky whispers through wax and apples passed blues.

All human faces seen are now fitted-well tailored flesh with often overwhelmed hearts tortuously meshed, vortexes, within the presence of my gest, everlasting enthusiasms, detangling, abreast, as former impressions once left – now only savored Saturnalia reveling in my psyche's ambrosial nests, and to some like webs for pests.

Enthralled, yesss, once HER purring nimbus burns humming – Her comeliness enslaves the profane pioneer; now, buzzing in Bacchilian splendor... the Mistress of all cataclysms incensed, with head thrown violently orgasmically backward – eyes-glazed beaming crimson SHE despairingly hissed – "glamour is everything to the downtrodden city amiss now pissed."

Periwinkle's penitential pious purple is profaned wherever disorder's cognitive-dissonance thrives and dishonesty's discord aboard is thus harbored collectively in accord. And so fell the blinding-blur of violet vestments kissed to the icy-cold grounds of northern lands once missed lost now defrosted found freed and unbound. For the "wretched refuse" and "tempest-tossed" – the "Mother of Exiles" and keeper of the lightening – inviting the lost – SHE both beckons all and only one, the just.

Robert Angelo Dalla Valle

Tribe of Black Boar ♠

Temple of the Trouncer ▲

T.O.T.T. of T.O.B.B. – ©2013

"Nature often uses illusions of this sort in order to accomplish its secret purposes. The true goal is covered over by a phantasm. We stretch out our hands to the latter, while nature, aided by our deception, attains the former. In the case of the Greeks it was the "will" wishing to behold itself in the work of art, in the transcendence of genius; but in order so to behold itself its creatures had first to view themselves as glorious, to transpose themselves to a higher sphere, without having that sphere of pure contemplation either challenge them or upbraid them with insufficiency. It was in that sphere of beauty that the Greeks saw the Olympians as their mirror images; it was by means of that aesthetic mirror that the Hellenic "will" opposed suffering and the somber wisdom of suffering which always accompanies artistic talent. As a monument to its victory stands Homer, the naïve artist." —By Friedrich Nietzsche from The Birth of a Tragedy – Walter Kaufmann translation.

Depth Aphotic: Androctonus - Third Totem- ©2012

Automatic drawing: Classification B – VIII/VI. Medium: Originally captured in green calligraphy pen ink on white parchment, now, here in

2013, presented in lavender on black exclusively for readers of *Sabbatica*, Ne-philim Press.

Due to limited space here, complete bibliographies, footnotes and oth-er organized relevant information is necessarily reserved for my full length works, beginning with The Enchiridions of a Black Eremite: Volume One: A Contemporary Study in Mediumistic Automatism as an Initiatory Vehicle: Pylon 0-1.

Nevertheless – briefly and noteworthy:

Endnotes

1. As defined: "The empirical method is generally characterized by the col-lection of a large amount of data before much speculation as to their signif-icance, or without much idea of what to expect, and is to be contrasted with more theoretical methods in which the collection of empirical data is guided largely by preliminary theoretical exploration of what to expect. The empir-ical method is necessary in entering hitherto completely unexplored fields, and becomes less purely empirical as the acquired mastery of the field in-creases. Successful use of an exclusively empirical method demands a higher degree of intuitive ability in the practitioner." – Source: Percy W. Bridgman, Gerald Holton, "Empirical Method."

The Empirical Method – as defined above; – Note; data, their signifi-cance, expectation, theoretical and then into "unexplored fields" in pursuit of total "mastery" and most significantly, this "demands a higher degree of intuitive ability in the practitioner." – These characteristically closely paral-lel components of my own empirical methods of randomized articulations and "drawing-lots"; with the exception that, the only "intention" I may ever employ is to be unguided therefore Untainted by other collective and indi-vidual human theory or previously paved perceptions as "theoretical" paths, as methods; so restrictive and tainting to one's purity of intuition and per-ception so very often are they. No scientific method beyond the complete mastery of the self, via intuition under will, is necessary. – In fact, I "back-track" later, after the fact, rather than am I ever initially guided by man's soporiferous socially-approved accoutrements.

My lifelong ever-evolving methods, of which, unlike the traditional scientist, utilize intuition wholly throughout every single creative and ex-ploratory process from the subjectively initial experience, to the publicly pragmatically empirical evolving into the potentially objective confirmation of the experiment therefore, "mastering the field"; as our machetes trailblazing new paths beyond the final frontiers. Nearly all of my creative "actions" are far from ever an impulsive guess, never impatient neither nor doubtful are they oppressed, however entirely automatic nonetheless, thus everything is received by blood be blessed. Very early-on, this then also intuitively, naturally matured (mutated) necessitating the inception and perpetually evolving sufficient methodologies, models, tools and sciences of exploring that which is perpetually received. As a metaphysically-endocrinological forty-plus year physiological engineered transparent-force of action, a vital intercessor and extension as metaphysical appendage or glandular of creative transmission protruding from the aura in-to the aether, the effective balance of which sustained requiring varieties of passion uncontained. Regarding my own scientific methods of experimental and applied (esoteric) sciences, the aforementioned is an extremely accurate though briefly defining synopsis in which my aim as intuitive creator-practitioner-scientist-skeptic, within this context, involves absolutely no expectation of the observer's experience, positive, negative or lack thereof. Seek no societal justifications of (perception-altering) theoretical pre-exploration as reassuring guide. Instead (remove the training-wheels), self-empowered systematically further enable the vehicle and utilize intuition as the very initiatory means and catalyst by which to pursue, gauge and either confirm or debunk any theory; with highly practical backward-winding reverse forms of divinatory resolution. My science or (what is labeled as) sorcery are, sans bells and whistles, the natural "Arts and Sciences of the Truths of Nature."

The (enabling) basic results (as expectation) in pursuance of par excellence exploring the (viable) "perceptibility" nature and potentiating probability of my intuitions, their experiences and the subsequently-resultant empirical methods necessary to further evoke (surf) such paths of sybaritic seraphical sentinels and diabolical denizens, to constrain and deeply explore them, and (optimistically-speaking) perhaps your own, are revealed amid my mediumistic automatic creations as a wide variety of writings, drawings, paintings, poems and sculptures in-practice elucidating my exercises, as the now refined and catalogued cumulative end result having mounted – the full devotional processes retrieved, extracted and documented, from the intimate initial pythonic trance-transition into transmission to the ontological phantasmagorically constrained, guided to final fruition of which, are housed, expounded and espoused within my enchiridions aflame. My neoteric empirical methods applied to the "Contemporary Study of Medium-istic Automatism as an Initiatory Vehicle" introduces an original, practical and essential tool as modern exposition, in Volume One of my Enchiridions of a Black Eremite; totally unrestricted thus intuitively highly eclectic.

2. Environmental, sociocultural circumstance, mimesis and the "sense" of experience observed via the trial & error of the empirical scientific-method, their obvious economical, religiopolitical and culturally bias influences imitated, are NOT, as were previously and even still presumed and propagated, solely the factors, presently engendering one's "circumstances" – but it is now proven that biologically inherited traits previously unconfirmed, via genomic imprinting and our D.N.A.'s ever-winding paths, in synergy with the former, IS. – Rise of the holism of atavism.

3. Regardless of any "source" of creative inspiration or purported epiphany and independently of commercial/industrial pursuits, an individual's arts may often subtly reflect the layering of the restrained and then very soon-after fleeting motifs and qualities of any great etheric liaison of love or ephemeral emissary of ecstasy always resonating forever entangled, re-arriving or respectfully resounding, returning reformed thus reaffirming, communicating, randomly navigating always anew within the vessel as tangible atavism. – By my definition and within this context, revealed via the greatest scientific-genetic breakthroughs of the last two decades, objectively, also realized subjectively biologically and highly esoterically; the atavism is an extension of or representation resultant from both the biological (epigenetics/genomic imprinting) and (into presently) non-biological (meme) elements dynamically and synergistically resurfacing, recalcitrant, refiltered, recalibrated for today thus refined, reflected and projected throughout the consciousness of the creator – redefined. – Literally Bridging the Physiological (past) TO the Metaphysical (present-future). The atavism now harnessed under will absolute.

4. Note that with regards to Themis (as Mother) and The Moirai, that in Hesiod, Theogony 211 ff (trans. Evelyn-White), the Moirai are also revealed to be the spawn of, in this particular, the virgin birth of Nyx, "though she lay with none", as quoted. Both 901 Re; Themis (whence within the poem which here redirects) and 211 noted here, are translations of Evelyn-White – and clear contradictions not uncommon within this context. Writers (especially later, post-Homer) inevitably became evermore (experienced) creatively indulgent

within the innately and uniquely human emotional chasm of the romanticism of theanthropism, or god-humanism, by placing the Moirai as either the daughters of Erebus/Nyx, Oceanus/Ge, Ananke, Necessity or Cronos/Nyx, as "the daughters of night" – of the primordial Nyx (night) whom Herself was the daughter of Khaos (air) and thus here replaces Themis (as Zeus' 2nd wife) as the Mother of the Fates – the "will" of whom none can escape, no mortal nor immortal – by some perspectives, not even Zeus; however by early Homeric account there is far less inflexibility as (a more humanized) Zeus both plays an active role in dishing out fate as well as can he (apparently rationalize/sympathize) determine to alter one's fate independently of all. As the actual god ruling of the fates, Zeus was known as Moiragetes meaning – leader of the fates.

The later and naturally evolving anthropomorphizing, as the human-quality of theanthropism, as an attribution of parents to these stereotypically ruthlessly perceived Moirai (collective-goddess-trinity-force of fate[s]), epitomizes sentimentalizing human-nature, however humanizing (cute), typically speaking, not that of the ancient Fathers' (especially not) Homer, Plato, Aeschylus nor Herodotus' sensibleness in logic; albeit Aeschylus' insistence upon strong spiritual affinities dominated, placing the divine entirely before the socioeconomic, which he never mentions particularly regarding Dike, yet just for one example, he did write of the "divine (theai)" as the Moirai and yet, having Nyx as their Mother, from Eumenides 961 ff, resultant from humanizing (meme) influences. Hesiod in Theogony eludes the following subject however Themis' role and existence, for the era, may well have been deemed simply necessary for Zeus, as mate, complimentary as consort. When Zeus unites with The Moirai, the event like all others is done for the citizen's benefit entirely, socioeconomic & human-interest, not necessarily logical, certainly not godlike. Such characteristics arriving within any creation are nearly inevitably reflective of the image, memes and perceptions of the creator. For Aeschylus with Eumenides 360 ff, and others, contradiction is also rampantly naturally-chaotically commonplace, as here he (Aeschylus) has the cooperation directed of the Olympians and Erinyes appointed by Zeus, rather than The Moirai thus contradicting himself; albeit granted, being related to all, Zeus was overused a tad and a "fill-in" of sorts, therefore, in actuality Aeschylus may have been inadvertently or perhaps simply deliberately, de-humanizing the Moirai, (rebalancing) having made them less communicative and socially inept without humane ambassadorial functionality by comparison to other fleeting notations, thus in essence restoring balance and elevating them more-so ambiguously divine and thus beyond the stoic stifling sophistic human condition. The profundity and perspicacity of such subtleties laced abound, as Spiritual Warriors escort truth, enabling those of the stone temples and celestial abodes far-reaching into new worlds and other dimensions. Hail Tahuti.

For what good in reason cometh of celestial sowed seed of gods to fields devolved likened unto man (?) – be not for delegation, communication, initiation, navigation of apotheosis and understanding in-communion without doubt neither hesitation.

Regardless of terminology used, therein the Olympian pantheon laid forces lurking which (self-replicated evolving to usurp) suppressed true "nature worship", instead, due to purported "progress" (poetry, philosophy and politics), the focus grew to become increasingly theanthropistic therefore driven towards the elevation of the human (ego) role within the pantheon itself, effectively humanizing gods and goddesses; no doubt the forces noted above are here benefactors in relation to the ego of man, as in concert, there is much to be unethically and unlawfully justified once the truth of divinity is rearranged corrupted-stained by the profane tainted principle, perception and memory of maniacal man deranged and shamed. Today, as positive progressive global example, the African Diaspora exemplifies the ever-evolving "balance" rather than the corruption of theanthropism when misappropriated, simply overused for convenience or the arrogance and greed of the smug and content. Animism, Totemism and Theanthropism are culturally creatively ever-present, today revivifying, reconstituting strong and resurrected as the "collective rise of the holism of the atavism" ushers empathy and progression. Optimistically speaking, theanthropism is simply a means by which to improve (communion) understanding, living, loving, dying, and renewal – the tools of the ambassador, ancestor and liaison. Mythological interpretative semantics and characteristically fleeting perceptions of the artist/writer/creator naturally develop and overlap, nonetheless, overall an identifiable (frequency) genesis having independently also arrived and evolving within early western ideologies emblematic of the nobility and impetus of the neoteric holy death folk religion/cults and its iconography. One of many such ancient Indo-European culturally "received" efficiency-molded truth and justice fueled religiously-philosophical and socially necessitated human/spirit constructs of fate, still very actively with us today – Necessary.

Hesiod, Theogony 211 ff (trans. Evelyn-White) (Greek epic C8th or C7th B.C.):

"And Nyx bare hateful Moros (Doom of Death) and black Ker (Fate of Death) and Thanatos (Death), and she bare Hypnos (Sleep) and the tribe of Oneiroi (Dreams). And again the goddess murky Nyx, though she lay with none, bare Momos (Criticism) and painful Oizys (Misery), and the Hesperides (Evenings) . . . Also she bare the Moirai (Fates) and the ruthless avenging Keres (Deaths) . . . Also deadly Nyx bare Nemesis to afflict mortal men, and after her, Apate (Deceit) and Philotes (Sex) and hateful Geras (Old Age) and hard-hearted Eris (Strife)."

Nyx, Dark Mother of Hypnos, Thanatos, the Tribe of Oneiroi, the Erinyes/Arai-Curses and the torch-bearing Hekate – the "daughter of great-bosomed Nyx." – The latter according to Bacchylides/Fragment 1b.

ETYMOLOGY

5. The Greek Moirai: PEPRO'MENE (Peprômenê), namely etopa, that is, the share destined by fate, occurs also as a proper name in the same sense as Moira or Fate. (Paus. viii. 21. § 2; Hom. Il. iii. 309.) Source: Dictionary of Greek and Roman Biography and Mythology. – The Moirai, Moirae' or Moerae, in Greek Μοῖραι – from moros (doom-fate, destiny), and from (era : ca. 800–100 BC) Ancient Doric Greek meiresthai – to "receive one's share" and correspondingly-equal to the Roman Parcae, the personification of destiny or as the sparing-ones, Fata/fate and by some accounts (Tibullus i. 8. 1. and Ovid ad Liv. 239), all Three "spin." The latter no surprise, when all three are also acting collectively as one, and considering the instinctive transcultural necessity of "spinning", from the Whirling Dervishes to the Ba Gua Daoist. Also, equaling the omnipotent maiden giantess trio of the Germanic Norns, which here specifically includes – 1. Urðr, 2. Verðandi and 3. Skuld – whose collective natures as Fates were also woven intertwined, becoming, the latter, a term also as ancient verb and concept at the root of each of their names. The Old Norse verb verða, "to become", is the etymological source of 1. Urðr-past-tense – "became" and 2. Verðandi-present-tense – "happening", with 3. Skuld, of the verb skole/skulle translated as "need to-shall be" or "that which should become-or-needs to be." Entangled-intertwined even ambiguously so, contrary to any "time" constructs, as collective – the Greek word moira (μοῖρα) = portion, as She partitions, collectively (as 3) as the matriarchal omnipresent "SHE" whom partitions thus apportioning, synergistically as, – the Greek "Fates" – Atropos (unturnable), Clotho (the

spinner) and Lachesis (the allotter). Their Roman Parcae equivalents accordingly Morta (death), Nona (ninth) and Decima (tenth), also correspond to the Etruscan Goddess of fate, Norita, the Roman Goddess Fortuna and also to the Roman Goddess of inevitability – Necessitas (the inescapable, her symbol the brazen-nail in use parallels that of the Greek life-thread spun), to the Lithuanian materialistic fate Goddess Dalia and the Lithuanian/Latvian Laima a.k.a. Laime and/or Laimas māte in Latvian – three in one, deemed "the three Laimas", as with Her two sisters Dēkla and Kārta, whom like the Moirai and Norns express their benevolence as patronesses of childbirth, also shape the necessary trinity of their fate's divine efficiency, as personifications of life, death and luck. And onto the Greek Goddess of all Fates, Ananke/Anance, the epitome of "scientific determinism", and corresponding to the Avestan Asha (aša) or Arta, as the unalterable impetus and necessity of natural fate and force of destiny, order, truth, balance, harmony, law, justice and thus constrain, as Necessity. Efficiency and Truth are ever-present themes propelling the pursuits of such developing necessity. From the macrocosmically universal balance, justice, virtue, order and truth of the Greek God Nereus, the ostrich feather of truth (Shu feather) set against the heart (soul [Ka]) upon the scales of the Egyptian Goddess Ma'at and then via Maat Kheru, if "justified", entering the Duat – (or just winning a civil trial), to the Vedic Rta (true) "order and truth", to the "order and truth" of the Avestan moral code's Zoroastrian "confessional concept" of their truth and righteousness theological sphere of aša/arta; respectively the Vedic (rta) and Avestan (arta) via lexicon and ideology are repeatedly paralleled as the source and path of truth historically and transculturally within expression, conduct, etymologically and here as defined: The Avestan aša/arta = "truth", which corresponding to and translated into the Vedic haithya = "true" – and the polar opposite of both rta/ haithya and aša/arta, of which for both being druj, is also within both lexicons translated into the term "lie." Serving the maintenance of the integrity and necessity of truth and justice, mortals as well as deities maintain a minimal influence upon these fates and at the moment of death, fate itself extinguishes as the Moirai become the Moirai Thanatoio/or Danatoio, "goddesses of death." In contrast for some, to the inevitable end of life fate and Thanatos of the Moirai, here comparatively, is a less common example inclusive of Aphrodite; relative to the patronesses of childbirth as a fate and also a result of Eros, as is here indicated within the – Orphic Hymn 55 to Aphrodite (trans. Taylor) (Greek hymns C3rd B.C.

ROBERT ANGELO DALLA VALLE

to 2nd A.D.): "The triple Moirai (Fates) [as birth goddesses] are ruled by thy [Aphrodite's] decree [as the goddess of procreation], and all productions yield alike to thee." – Here the latter with intent, further establishes a clearly benevolent representation. Also relative here to Aphrodite is that the corresponding animal, unlike the white turtle dove of Demeter, Aphrodite and aspects of Safekh-Aubi and Sefekh (393), for the Moirai, is considered to be the more common dark-greyish turtle dove variant. The Fates also correspond to the Hesperides, or the "daughters of the evening star", their golden apples and enticing incitement of dark powers, misery, fate, and strife – via Eris (Strife) – came the infamous apple-spell, inscribed "For the Fairest", which effectively precipitated the Trojan War.

6. Vedic Sanskrit and Avestan/Old Iranian – very fruitful siblings, the former is the eldest originating from the latter's Indo-European comprised fragments of linguistic-reconstruction. Both etymologically, as interpreted here, embrace closely evolving variants; such as old Sanskrit's Atharvan = fire-priest, of lightning, and Atharvans = priests of the celestial fire-god Atar, a.k.a. the lightening god, and in Persian Arthvan = priest, which then later becomes Brahmin or brahmana. Avesta priests prided themselves as Athravans or Atharvans, of the fire-cult; they who tended the sacred fire. Also, the fire gods Agni and Atharvan are both separate entities, and both are known as the Lord of Lightning. And as the earliest panacea as a form of the internal elixir of life and source of alchemical elixir vitae traditions of ascetic sages from India traced to China's Daoist's psychogenesis into Islam onto Europe and Roger Bacon; the Soma priests preparing the sacred entheogen-elixirs of immortality (of Amanita muscaria) to commune with the gods, were also known as Atharvan(s). "Atharvan" is also revered as the Indian equivalent and actual origin of the Prometheus archetype. The Avestan key component of Asha corresponds to the Sanskrit root "RTA" delineating the "eternal law and order" of the Righteousness and universal law of Truth. And the Avestan aša/arta (or asha) which = "truth", in English is "Asha" and = 'Esh (or aish - אש) in Hebrew which = fire, and which is 'Eshsha' or 'Eshsh in Chaldean (cf Sanskrit ush to burn) and = Asha, & Aram thus = Fire. Asha (cosmic-order) is also defined as wish and as Hope used as a commonly given feminine name, it's also translated to life in Swahili and to some Hindus it is "gift from the gods" – as ASHA (आशा): The Indian derived term from Sanskrit आशा (asha) meaning wish, desire, and hope, therefore clearly displaying how these conclusive similarities also include mimesis. Promethean

–196–

precursors prospered and proliferated. Here, collectively and individually simultaneously fluid animations as vitally iconic actions within Malkuth as cultural and astrally-symbiotic manifestations outside of "time" and/or evolving as icons serving as necessities of universal Efficiency, for "order" and morally, elementally as deities, ideologically; their intrinsic origins are also all-inclusive of the "biological" – epigenetics, thus invariably universally-collective forces as concrete blood transmissions – transcendent all manner and matter of space-time, culture and perhaps even initial intention of man. Truth and Justice are here ablaze via the individual, the priest, with the divine, quite synonymous with the dynamism of the eternal blood of Fire. Also relevant to asha/esh; Note: From Easton's 1897 Bible Dictionary: Eshbaal man of Baal, the fourth son of king Saul (1 Chr. 8:33; 9:39). He is also called Ish-bosheth (q.v.), 2 Sam. 2:8. Also, noted in Smith's Bible Dictionary as: (Baal's man), (1 Chronicles 8:33; 9:39) the same as Ish-bosheth. And lastly, from Hitchcock's Bible Names Dictionary (late 1800's): Esh-baal, the fire of the idol, or of the ruler.

By efficiently eternal flames' (lightening-fire) truth's (eternal law) our ancestor's (priest's) word in blood resurrected forevermore reigns.

7. The Avestan deity Mithra (i.e. covenant/contract) is an impenetrable enforcer-god of the integrity of law whom consequently preserves/protects aša/arta exactly as the Rig Vedic Mitra also preserves/protects rtá – therefore they're nevertheless independent/self-reliant yet too simultaneously intertwined, collectively entangled – as they're indistinguishably serving – preserving and protecting – the same precise current(s)/force(s) of truth indeed evolving as does the elegant all-enabling & often overwhelming construed truths of the Egyptian Goddess Ma'at. Truth is therefore exoterically, esoterically, historically and culturally both subjectively and objectively transmitted thus categorically breeching all boundaries – universally received, physiologically, metaphysically and space-time independent. – *Additional bibliographical sources for number Five, Six and Seven (in Etymology) also include; "Civilization of the Eastern Irānians in Ancient Times: The Old Irānian..." By Dr. Wilhelm Geiger, translated from German by Darab-Dastur Peshotan Sanjānā, London, 1886. "The Journal of the Royal Asiatic Society of Great Britain & Ireland", London, 1893. "History of Zoroastrianism" by Dhalla, Maneckji Nusservanji, New York, 1938 and "Heraclitus and Iran", History of Religions by Duchesne-Guillemin, Jacques, 1963.

8. Re; Greek Atropos: in Greek Ἄτροπος, "without turn" (meaning She cannot be turned or avoided, and not contrary to spinning), was the inflexible one and eldest of the Moirai trio – and from Hesiod, Shield of Heracles 258 ff (trans. Evelyn-White) (Greek epic C8th or 7th B.C.): "Klotho (Clotho) and Lakhesis (Lachesis) stood over them, and smaller than they was Atropos, no tall goddess, yet she it is who is eldest of them, and ranked high beyond the two others." – SHE is unequalled, our Lady. Uniquely paralleling Atropos is the Lithuanian Goddess of death Giltinė the Reaper – a.k.a. Kaulinyčia, Maras and black-death/plague – Her totem the owl, She is associated with Laima (fate/luck) as a sister. Correspondingly also is the Roman Morta, to the Roman "original" Goddess Fortuna Primigenia and to the Etruscan winged-goddess version of Athrpa, the latter also using the hammer & nail, thus influential to the later Roman Goddess Necessitas. – Atropos = cannot be turned, and had in various accounts possessed either a sundial, the scroll, a wax tablet, or the scales, and is exclusively depicted as the "fate" with shears whom actually quantifies and determines all circumstance of death and a "Holy Death", by cutting the figurative thread of one's life solely unassisted, as of the three, Clotho = spinner and had just a spindle thus She only spun this thread and Lachesis = disposer of lots, whom held a staff/scepter, directing it to the horoscope, and She merely measured the thread of life. Woman of the just blade, ways of the Old Norse – "becoming", path of the sickle-green, warrior and harvester of souls.

Atropos is also the origin of the natural entheogen and medicinal tropane alkaloid genus of the Solanaceae family, termed Atropine; – extracted from mandrake, belladonna/deadly nightshade, angel's trumpets, datura, all eleven species of henbanes and many others. This Solanaceae (deadly nightshade/solanum-potato) family also involves an exquisitely broad range of (40+) genera which includes potatoes, capsicum/chili pepper, tomatoes, eggplant and tobacco, to the longevity-boosting super-antioxidant wolfberry and the once thought to have been extinct now critically endangered species of M. begoniifolia of the genus Mellissia. From ancient to modern times, the agriculturally necessary, nourishing and essentially edible, to the metaphysical, to medicinal, the clinical, critical, or for the beautician, to the witch or shaman, Solanaceae was and is an all-encompassing family of botanical bliss.

"All things are poison and nothing (is) without poison; only the dose makes that a thing is no poison." —Paracelsus, 1493-1541

"Nox approaches: a garland of poppies binds her peaceful brow, black Somnia trail her." Ovid, Fasti 4. 661 ff (trans. Boyle) (Roman poetry C1st B.C. to C1st A.D.)

This concludes;
An Automatic Writing
The Poem
-Provocation: Justitia Omnibus-

Holistic Healthcare Has No Obstacle
"Bridging the Physiological TO the Metaphysical" – providing an eclectic range of holistic health services to thousands of individual clients for over 20 years, ensuring success and longevity via the consistency of professionalism, integrity, safety, results, empathy, discretion and confidentiality.

For private-individual or group consultation and other various physiological or metaphysical services inquiries, email: rdallavalle@optonline.net or contact Robert privately on Facebook regarding any questions that you may have, whether your goals are Physical or Metaphysical.

Forthcoming 2013 – The Enchiridions of a Black Eremite: Volume One: A Contemporary Study in Mediumistic Automatism as an Initiatory Vehicle: Pylon 0-1 – including the treatise and art – 393 Sefekh, the Consort of Thoth – excerpts including various art of which, may be found in the Qliphoth Opus I Esoteric Publication and Qliphoth Opus II Esoteric Publication.

The E.B.E. – A serious modern-day inquiry and initiatory journey spanning several decades into neither-neither realms of trance induction including oneirophrenia and endocrinology to entheogens and psychology utilized in ritualistic mediumistic automatism creative ventures, employing various systems of sexual magick, Orgone and the renascence of the atavism. Oneirocritical-oneiromantic traditional to contemporary solitary initiations and critical explorations into the anthropology of art and religion including animism, totemism and anthropomorphism via epistemology, cosmology and ontology, with veneration are observed. ♦

Love,
Robert Angelo Dalla Valle

Labels only afford the comfort of knowing, where intuition has failed to have been received.

To "doubt" another is the way of the self-saboteur as well. All doubt is deception; know this in all ways, always.

Pomba Gira da Calunga © - One third of a triptych - Automatic drawing - Classification A: III Reserved/gift and here depicted within an initial thus transitory and unrefined state revealed only via pen-etched India ink and machete-etched blood, later misted with coffee, espresso, various rums, rosewater & honey, with Love, upon Southworth fine coral parchment, 8.5" x 11".

All concepts and creations, written and visual - ©Robert Angelo Dalla Valle - ©1971-2013

-Love, R.A.D. ∞
XXX

-Robert Angelo Dalla Valle - all creations ©1971-2013

CONTRIBUTORS

Orryelle Defenestrate-Bascule
www.facebook.com/orryelle.defenestratebascule
www.crossroads.wild.net.au
www.crossroads.wild.net.au/esoterotica.htm

Ljóssál Loðursson
www.facebook.com/profile.php?id=649260902
www.ophiolatreia.org
OrdoNigriSolis@hotmail.com

Magick Kazim
www.facebook.com/renaissance.kazim
www.kazim-renaissance.fr
www.dark-shaman.com
kazim_azylum@hotmail.com

Hermeticusnath (Aion 131)
www.facebook.com/aion.hermeticusnath
www.psychicsophia.com/globalritualism.html
aion@psychicsophia.com

Robert Angelo Dalla Valle
www.facebook.com/robert.dallavalle
rdallavalle@optonline.net

S Ben Qayin
http://www.facebook.com/sben.qayin
s.benqayin@ymail.com

Hagen von Tulien

www.facebook.com/hagen.von.tulien
www.behance.net/Hagen_von_Tulien
www.voudongnosis.org
www.ega.kosmic-gnosis.org
hagen93@online.de

Nicholaj De Mattos Frisvold

www.facebook.com/nicholaj.frisvold
www.starrycave.com
nicholaj@gmail.com

Bradley Allen Bennett

www.facebook.com/bradley.a.bennett.1
ducorvi@yahoo.com

Kyle Fite

www.facebook.com/kyle.fite.58
www.starfirepublishing.co.uk/
www.facebook.com/pages/Noctuas-Nest/619128734769260
kylefite@yahoo.com

Cláudio Carvalho

http://www.facebook.com/claudiocesardecarvalho93
www.sociedadelamatronika.blogspot.com
www.kennethgrant.blogspot.com
claudiocarvalho93@gmail.com

Dante Miel

www.facebook.com/BlackSunHorizons
www.facebook.com/dante.miel
www.barnesandnoble.com/w/
breaking-the-rules-of-magic-dante-miel/1114892193
dantemiel1@me.com

Sean Woodward

www.facebook.com/seanofficial

www.gothick.co.uk
t3kton@gmail.com

Vaenus Obscvra
www.facebook.com/ars.v.obscvra
ars.v.obscvra@hotmail.com

Andrew Dixon/Sahra Price
www.facebook.com/andimoon

Edgar Kerval
www.facebook.com/edgar.kerval
www.sunbehindthesun.blogspot.com
www.qliphothjournal.blogspot.com
www.soundcloud.com/theredpath
www.facebook.com/sabbaticagrimoire
kerval111@gmail.com

~fin~

Lightning Source UK Ltd.
Milton Keynes UK
UKOW02f2011251016

286146UK00004B/333/P